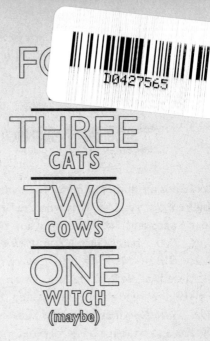

FO...

THREE CATS

TWO COWS

ONE WITCH (maybe)

'Not only one of the best Irish children's books of the year, but I honestly think one of the best Irish children's books we've ever had, full stop ... It's an amazingly clever book.'
ROBERT DUNBAR, *The Gay Byrne Show*

Special Merit Award to The O'Brien Press *from* **Reading Association of Ireland**
'for exceptional care, skill and professionalism in publishing, resulting in a consistently high standard in all of the children's books published by The O'Brien Press'

SIOBHÁN PARKINSON

Siobhán is the author of many prize-winning books for children. *Sisters ... No Way!* won the Bisto Book of the Year Award and *The Moon King* and *Four Kids, Three Cats, Two Cows, One Witch (maybe)* have both received Bisto Merit Awards. *Call of the Whales* was shortlisted for the Reading Association of Ireland 2001. For younger readers she has written *The Leprechaun Who Wished He Wasn't* and *All Shining in the Spring*. She has also written a book for older readers, *Breaking the Wishbone,* which has been widely acclaimed. Siobhán lives in Dublin with her wood-turner husband, Roger Bennett, and her schoolgoing son, Matthew.

FOUR KIDS
THREE CATS
TWO COWS
ONE WITCH
(maybe)

SIOBHÁN PARKINSON

THE O'BRIEN PRESS
DUBLIN

First published 1997 by The O'Brien Press Ltd.,
20 Victoria Road, Rathgar, Dublin 6, Ireland.
Tel: +353 1 4923333; Fax: +353 1 4922777
E-mail: books@obrien.ie
Website: www.obrien.ie
Reprinted 1998 (twice), 1999, 2000, 2002.

ISBN: 0-86278-515-4

British Library Cataloguing-in-Publication Data
Parkinson, Siobhan
Four Kids, three cats, two cows, one witch (maybe)
1. Children's stories
I. Title
823.9'14 [J]

6 7 8 9 10
02 03 04 05

The O'Brien Press receives
assistance from

The Arts Council
An Chomhairle Ealaíon

Typesetting, editing, layout, design: The O'Brien Press Ltd.
Cover separations: C&A Print Services Ltd.
Printing: Cox & Wyman Ltd.

CONTENTS

AUTHOR'S NOTE

In most cultures, when children reach the age of around twelve or fourteen, there is some sort of ceremony to mark their transition from childhood to young adulthood. In Ireland, most children are confirmed between the ages of about eleven and fifteen, depending on the church they belong to, and Jewish boys have their Bar Mitzvah at the age of thirteen. These are examples of transitional ceremonies to mark the change that is taking place in young people at the threshold of adulthood.

In some cultures young people who are approaching adulthood have to undergo some sort of test or ordeal. They might have to go off by themselves into the forest, for example, and survive on their own initiative. In other cultures the transition is marked by the older people telling the children the secret stories of their tribe. Once they have these stories, they are no longer children, but grown-up members of the tribe.

But no matter what form these ceremonies and rituals take (and in some cultures they are pretty nasty) every child has to make the journey from childhood to young adulthood for himself or herself.

Chapter 1

PERSUADING ELIZABETH

ISLANDS DON'T JUST APPEAR, hovering up greenly out of the sea like the back of some monster of the deep, giving a long, slow heave. Beverley knew that. She knew the island had always been there. It was just that she'd never taken all that much notice of it before.

As a general rule, Beverley did notice things. She liked to take a mental snapshot of her surroundings, wherever she was, and file it all away for future reference, and she'd done exactly that with Tranarone the first day they arrived, a week ago. She didn't think much of Tranarone, actually. It wasn't much of a place. Or maybe she was just growing out of seaside holidays. When she was small, she used to love them, when they all went on holiday together as a family and had fun in a family sort of way, playing frisbee on the beach and poking in the rock pools and trailing flimsy pink fishing nets on bamboo stems along the sea floor and never catching anything more interesting than a few broken shells and a length of slimy green seaweed and having sandy picnics when the sun shone. All that had changed since her older brothers had grown up and gone off to boring old university and left her behind to go on dreary holidays alone with her parents while they went Inter-Railing across Europe for the summer. To make things worse, her parents were going through one of their sticky patches at the moment, squabbling, scoring points off each other, being perfect pigs.

On the day she really noticed the island properly for the first time, Beverley was mooching slowly along the cold beach – it was often quite cold in June, though sometimes you got these tantalising flashes of hot weather that made you think maybe there was going to be a summer after all – dragging a long, damp, rather unpleasant-smelling piece of brown seaweed, like a broad leather belt, which she'd picked up half-heartedly and now felt illogically guilty about dropping, as if it were a piece of litter. There wasn't much to see on the beach, and she'd been over it all a hundred times before, collected all the different sorts of shells there were and classified them and noted them down neatly in her Seashore Habitat notebook, examined every last rockpool endlessly, though she knew perfectly well that there was only ever one sort of sea anemone on Irish beaches – the translucent red kind that looked like a half-melted raspberry fruitgum – and clambered over all the rocks and tried, unsuccessfully, to pick limpets off them.

The sun was shining very brightly, though it wasn't giving much heat, so brightly that when Beverley raised her eyes from the beach and glanced out to sea, she was forced to put her hand up to her forehead in a peak to protect them from the glare of the sun. Perhaps it was because she squinted under the visor she made of her hand that she focused more intensely than usual on the island, lying quietly out there in the bay. In any case, whatever the reason, the island seemed at that moment to catch her attention, almost as if it had moved, or waved at her.

It was an ordinary enough little island, if islands can ever be counted ordinary, not very large, but a good size all the same. It wasn't the rocky and uninviting sort of island you sometimes see jutting aggressively out of the sea. In fact, it looked a bit like a piece of the mainland that was somehow left over. It was as if some giant child had put it aside in puzzlement, unable to find a place for it in the enormous jigsaw of the west coast of Ireland.

Beverley shook herself, like a wet dog, as if to shake off this silly idea. Islands weren't bits of jigsaw puzzles. They were perfectly explicable natural phenomena. That's what they were. Yes. You could read about them in geography books. They were caused by continental shifts or they were the tips of undersea mountains or something.

And yet this island didn't look a bit like a phenomenon in a geography book. It looked like a lost, homeless, thrown-aside bit of the countryside. It seemed to Beverley that it longed to be visited, as if it were lonely out there in the sea, cut off from its rightful place in the world. She shook herself again. What was coming over her?

All the same, she reasoned, it would be nice to take a trip out to the island. She could explore it, map it maybe. Perhaps there would be more interesting rock pools out there, or caves, or the sort of beach pebbles you saw in colourful books about the seashore that when you split them open turn out to have semi-precious insides you can polish to spectacular effect, or sea-urchins, maybe, or starfish – all those pretty things you never did find on real seashores no matter how hard you looked.

You wouldn't need a boat or anything. You could wade out to the island at low tide. The island was only a short distance off-shore, a splashy, squelchy paddle-walk.

But this trip wasn't going to be just a walk. This was going to be a proper expedition, an investigative journey, a voyage of exploration. In her excitement, Beverley dropped the piece of seaweed she had been dragging, and set off away from the beach towards the village, such as it was – two shops, two pubs, and a small restaurant with a takeaway window.

She would need to plan this expedition. Beverley believed in doing things properly. She never just launched into a project. She liked to write things down, make lists, approach things logically. She wouldn't be rushed. Thinking how very admirable an approach to adventure this was, what a very organised and wholly sensible person she was, Beverley turned her sandalled feet, blue with cold and gritty with sand, into the Spar-shop-cum-post-office, which, together with the poky little old-fashioned, beer-and-ham-smelling pub-cum-grocery next door, served the daily needs of Tranarone's holiday visitors and local people.

They kept things like pens and paper at the back of the shop, near the post-office section, next to an unbelievably awful selection of birthday cards, all roses and kittens for the ladies and fishing rods and sports cars for the gents. There wasn't much choice in the pen and paper department either: Bic ballpoints in red or blue; A.W. Faber pencils, yellow, HB, with the tops already pointed so that they were like vicious little ice-picks; plastic pencil-parers, also red and blue, like the ballpoints; Belvedere Bond writing paper, but only in the small size, and lined; rather enticing-looking thin airmail envelopes, like tissue-paper, with green and orange edging and a picture of an aeroplane in the corner and *Par Avion/Aerphost* printed underneath, but no matching airmail paper. Beverley flicked through the lined writing paper speculatively. This wasn't really what she wanted. But there weren't any notebooks, just school copybooks, squared for sums and red-and-blue-lined for practising joined-up writing. She poked around a bit more, hoping to find something more suitable.

Her hand, burrowing under the copies, closed over something that was the right shape. She pulled it out. It was nice and stout and it had a handsome red cover with a watery look, like a taffeta dress Beverley's older cousin had worn to her Debs, but when she opened it, it was the wrong sort of notebook, with vertical red rules, for doing accounts or something of that sort. Irritably, she tossed it aside.

'Hey, there! No need to break the place up!'

The words were cross, but the tone of voice was amused, teasing. It was Kevin, the shopkeeper's eldest son. Beverley knew him to see. He was nearly always in the shop, helping his mother, or else you could hear his voice coming from the living quarters at the back, where he was minding the younger ones, cooking them their tea or shouting at them to get into their pyjamas. He was tall, and wore a leather jacket, and thought he was just It. That's what came of being the eldest and being looked up to all the time.

With a sigh, Beverley picked up a sum copy and walked to the cash register, pointedly ignoring Kevin.

Mrs Mulrooney was busy packing a cardboard box with groceries, and totting up the items as she went, reading half-aloud from a grubby little list and shaking her head disapprovingly. Beverley looked around to see whose groceries these were, but there were no other customers in the shop. Mrs Mulrooney must be making up an order.

'Ninety-five,' muttered Mrs Mulrooney. 'One-oh-six. Thirty-six. Seventy-two. Six jars of honey (*six* jars this time? hm) at ninety-five pence, five pounds seventy. Forty-five.'

Beverley could see she was going to be ages. She started to tap her foot impatiently, flapping the copybook up and down in time with her irritation. Suddenly, on an up-flap, she felt the copybook being taken out of her hand. She swirled around, to see Kevin at her elbow, copybook in hand.

'I'll take for this,' he offered. 'Save you the wait. Twenty-five pee please.'

Beverley despised people who said 'pee' for pence. She twitched her nose and handed over the money without a word. Kevin was already on the other side of the counter and was rolling up the copybook into a tube to stuff it into a thin white plastic bag.

'I won't be needing *this*,' said Beverley disdainfully, shaking the copybook out of the plastic bag again, and hoping she was getting a whole lecture on green economics into her voice.

'That's all right,' said Kevin cheerfully, as if she had apologised for something. His teeth were remarkably straight and even, and his dark hair was flicked to the side so that you could see the expensive layering in it, each hair apparently individually cut and arranged. 'Getting ready for going back to school already? You must be a very keen student.'

Ha-ha.

'No,' said Beverley coldly, not explaining why she wanted the copybook.

'Ah well!' Kevin shrugged his shoulders. His underlip puckered as he spoke. It was a deep rose colour. Then he smiled, for no apparent reason, and Beverley could see a flash of those even teeth, very white against that rosy underlip.

'I was looking for a notebook, actually,' Beverley relented.

'Oh, sorry about that,' said Kevin. 'We ordered some yesterday, but they won't be here for another day or two.'

Well, he was trying to be nice. At least he was civil. Beverley ventured a small smile as she pocketed her change. She shouldn't have. He took advantage of her good nature and gave a distinct wink. Beverley turned away quickly to hide her hot cheeks. How dare he! She ran out of the shop, the door clanging dementedly behind her.

She raced along the unevenly tarmacked road till she reached the holiday cottage. By the time she arrived, her cheeks were burning with exertion instead of embarrassment. She flopped onto her bed and took some deep breaths before she opened the sum copy and began to write.

This is what she wrote on the smooth, clean surface of the first page:

Purpose of expedition: To explore Lady Island under the following headings: geography, geology, flora, fauna, ecology, miscellaneous.
Explorers: Beverley Wilson (leader); Elizabeth Ryan; Gerard O'Connor.

'*Requirements*,' she wrote next, and went on to list everything she could think of:

> *Torch and batteries*
> *String*
> *Notebook and pencil*
> *Matches*
> *Penknife*
> *Provisions*
> *Rug*
> *Warm jackets and spare socks*
> *Chocolate*

I should've been a boy-scout, she thought with satisfaction and wiggled her cold toes inside her sandals. Flares, she thought. We could do with those, for emergencies. But what exactly were flares? What did they look like, and where did you get them? She shrugged, but added this item to her list anyway. She'd think of something.

She closed the sum copy and slithered off her duvet. Now to find Elizabeth, who'd moved into one of the horrible holiday bungalows up the lane last week. Elizabeth would be sure to think this was a great idea.

'I don't know,' said Elizabeth Ryan, slowly, shaking her long pale plait so that it swung from shoulder-blade to shoulder-blade.

The two girls were sitting at the round, brown, Formica-topped table in the bungalow, eating raspberry ripple ice cream out of breakfast cereal bowls with vacuous pink flowers on them, like no flowers that had ever existed in the wild or in a garden.

'Why not?'

'I don't know,' Elizabeth repeated, licking her spoon thought-fully and squinting at the inverted image of herself in it. 'There's something about that island. I don't know what it is. Someone lives there, I think.'

'So what, if someone lives there? It's hardly a crime to go and have a picnic there just because someone lives there. I mean, people live on Inishbofin and the Aran islands and all. That doesn't mean you can't go and take a look.'

'Well, it might be private property,' argued Elizabeth. 'It might be trespassing.'

'Oh trespassing! Who cares? I don't think you can really be

prosecuted for trespassing.'

'Prosecuted? You mean, court and that? God, I never thought of that.'

'No, dumbo, I mean *not* court and that. I mean, I don't think it actually is a crime to trespass, but anyway, that's not the point.'

'What *is* the point?' asked Elizabeth, gazing at Beverley. 'I forget.'

Elizabeth was such a dreamer! She couldn't concentrate from one end of a sentence to the other.

'The point is,' said Beverley, with exaggerated patience, 'are you going to come with me to explore the island or not?'

'But what if they don't want us there? Suppose they have a Doberman.'

'Here we go a-*gain*,' sighed Beverley. 'Suppose they have a tiger! Or a herd of elephants!'

'They couldn't – could they?' Elizabeth's mouth was opened in a big round O.

'Of course they couldn't, nitwit. Where's your spirit of adventure? Are you coming or not?'

'Well ...'

'OK,' said Beverley bossily, taking this for a Yes. 'Now, the thing is, do we take Gerard or not? I think we'd better have a boy, even if he's only a little squirt, for doing the dirty work, you know.'

'Oh yes,' Elizabeth agreed. She didn't have a high opinion of her cousin Gerard either, and she was quite happy to see him in the role of dirty-worker. Even as she said this, she realised that she had implicitly agreed to this expedition. Oh well, perhaps it would be fun. It would be better than sticking around cold and uneventful Tranarone anyway.

Elizabeth picked up her cereal bowl and started to lick the last of the ice cream off it, with long pink licks of her tongue. Beverley stared at her in wide-eyed disapproval for a moment. Then she picked up her own bowl with a giggle and started to do the same. It tasted better than off the spoon for some reason. Now, what could the scientific explanation for this be she wondered.

Chapter 2

PACKING

BEVERLEY HAD EVERYTHING UNDER CONTROL. The list in the sum copy was all ticked off, and she had distributed the items among the three of them. Gerard was going to have to carry all the uncomfortable and heavy things, like saucepans and cutlery, things that stuck out through your rucksack and prodded your back. (This was to punish him for being a boy.)

Beverley had the food in her rucksack, as she was the cook as well as the leader, and cooks need to be in charge of the larder. They had tins of sardines, tuna and spaghetti – Gerard got to carry the tin-opener – and hard-boiled eggs still in their shells, teabags, a small carton of milk, cans of fizzy drinks, a large sliced pan, a quarter pound of sliced cooked ham and a quarter pound of something pink and also sliced called luncheon meat that Elizabeth had persuaded Beverley (who was a food snob, and hadn't much liked the idea of tinned spaghetti either) to agree to, a packet of rashers and a packet of sausages, a ring of black pudding, a small jar of baby beetroots from Poland, a tube of Pringles crisps and a large foil bag of peanuts. They also had a plastic basket of pears, two bunches of bananas, like half-clenched yellow baseball mitts, assorted packets of biscuits, a tin of peaches, a tin of pineapple rings and several large bars of chocolate. Beverley had wanted to bring a tin of condensed milk, because in all the best stories with picnics in them, they have condensed milk, but they only had evaporated milk in the Spar shop, and she wasn't sure if it was the same thing.

Beverley had wisely divided the chocolate into survival rations, not to be eaten unless there was an emergency, and ordinary chocolate for standard consumption. The emergency chocolate got wrapped in tinfoil and each person had to carry some of it separately.

'Flares,' said Elizabeth, laying the contents of her rucksack on the brown candlewick bedspread – why, Beverley wondered, for the umpteenth time, was every single thing in this house brown? – for a final check before packing it all away neatly again. 'We should have flares.'

Elizabeth was carrying all the non-culinary items – spare clothes, rugs, notebooks, compass, matches, the first aid kit and so forth, and so flares seemed to be part of her area of responsibility.

'I've thought of that,' said Beverley, producing two very long spindly coloured paper parcels with sticks out of the bottom, something like a cross between fishing rods and elongated lolli-pops.

'Is that what flares look like?' asked Elizabeth doubtfully, fingering the thin waxed paper.

Gerard looked at Beverley with wide eyes. He was rather in awe of this capable older girl. Only she could have thought of such an exotic-looking pair of items as part of the equipment for an adventure. He was sitting hunched on the floor with his knees under his chin, trying very hard to cough as quietly as possible, so as not to annoy the girls, and keeping well out of the way. Fat was snoring in the gap between his thighs and his chest.

It had been a mistake to bring Fat on holiday. Gerard's mother had been right about that. He had sulked all the way and peed through the wicker floor of the cat basket, all over the back seat of his uncle and aunt's Volvo. The stench was awful at the time, and it got worse as the holiday wore on. Every time the car door opened, the sweetish smell of stale cat pee assaulted everyone's nostrils, and they all turned to Gerard and said: 'You and that blinking cat! You can't take cats on holidays. Nobody does, in case you haven't noticed.'

Actually, they didn't all say that about Fat. His uncle and aunt were far too kind to make such hurtful remarks. They were nice to him because he was the child of a single mother. There were two sorts of people in the world, he found – the ones who despised you because your mother wasn't married, and the ones who bent over backwards to show you that they didn't disapprove one little bit, in fact they hadn't even noticed that you hadn't got a father, though now you came to mention it, right enough, there didn't seem to be an adult male in your household.

But Elizabeth had no such scruples, and she said it (about the blinking cat) loudly enough and often enough for three. Gerard held Fat in his arms and buried his face in his rancid, dirty-cream fur and said nothing when Elizabeth poured scorn on him, but his toes squirmed inside his runners.

Gerard had made a collar and lead for Fat out of wool. Cats are difficult on holiday at the best of times. They hate being away from home. But cats at the seaside are the end. They steal people's fish, and they hate water. Fat didn't like the collar. He probably thought he looked silly in it. He did. Very silly. So every time Gerard tried to put it on, Fat kicked up the most dreadful stink, hissing and snarling and scratching and doing a good imitation of a bridge with hair. Then he ran away and sulked under the knobbly brown furniture in the holiday bungalow.

In the end, Gerard gave up on the lead and carried Fat everywhere. People looked at him in amazement, a small, pale, underweight, asthmatic eleven-year-old whose ears stuck out and who wore glasses that looked too big for him, carrying a large, pale, overweight, possibly also eleven-year-old cat along the beach. But what could Gerard do? If he didn't carry him, Fat'd wander off and get lost. And he certainly wouldn't walk on the beach. He didn't like sand between his toes, and good gracious! there might be a damp bit.

'No,' Beverley was saying, from several feet above the crouching Gerard. 'These are garden candles, also called flares, but they're not really the distress kind. You see, you stick the pointy bit in the earth and you light this bit. You take the paper off first, of course. My parents bring them every year, in case we get barbecue weather. We never do.'

'They won't be much good in an emergency,' said Elizabeth. Elizabeth had a hunch there might just be an emergency. She had a funny feeling about this island that she couldn't quite put her finger on.

'Oh, I think they'll be visible from the land. Especially if we put them up on a hill or something.'

'Only if it's dark, you thick.'

'Umm,' said Beverley. She hadn't thought of that. Or rather, she had only thought of an emergency as being the kind of thing that happened at night. 'Oh well, we'd better take them anyway. They'll be better than nothing. You can carry them.'

'Gee thanks,' said Elizabeth. She sighed as she took the ridiculous things from Beverley. Really, Beverley could be a bit much at times. But still, maybe they would be better than nothing. Elizabeth stood the garden flares against the wall, ready to take next morning.

She caught sight of Gerard as she turned around. 'You're not bringing that cat, by the way,' she said. Elizabeth hated Fat almost as much as she despised her small boy cousin, and she had a theory that people with asthma shouldn't have cats anyway. Gerard lived in fear that his mother might get to hear about this theory, so he tried very hard to be nice to Elizabeth, just to make sure she didn't mention it some time, to get her own back on him. Not that she ever noticed how nice he was to her.

'But I have to,' he wailed now. 'If I leave him behind he'll panic and pee in the house. Or worse.'

'Worse?' squeaked Elizabeth. 'You mean ...?'

'Yes, I do,' said Gerard miserably. 'And if you think cat pee stinks, you should smell ...'

Actually, Gerard was quite fond of the smell of cat pee. It reminded him of flowering currant. But he knew from experience that other people didn't exactly see it that way.

'All right, all right,' said Elizabeth, adjusting the garden flares so they didn't slither over. She was beginning to wonder why she'd agreed to this expedition. Between Beverley with her stupid barbecue candles and Gerard with his endless wheezing and his ridiculous cat, they were going to be a right lot of eejits going off to the island. 'Don't go on! Boys are so revolting.'

Gerard thought this was a bit unfair. It was Fat's bad habits that were in question, not his, after all. But he didn't dare to irritate Elizabeth more than was strictly necessary.

'You'll have to carry your rucksack as well,' Elizabeth warned him.

'Sure. No problem.' Gerard was eager to co-operate, to make up for the cat.

Elizabeth started to pack her rucksack, calling out each item as she tucked it in. Beverley ticked everything off on the list for the second time, just to be sure they had everything. The list she'd begun with in the sum copy two days before had got much longer, and now included items like a magnifying glass and binoculars, and Elizabeth's rucksack was bulging by the time she'd finished. But it was neither as knobbly nor as heavy as Gerard's, so she didn't complain. Plus, she didn't have to carry a cat, so really she was doing pretty well.

'OK, so we're all set then, aren't we?' said Beverley. 'Are you sure you checked the time of the tide, Gerard?' She toed him in the behind to catch his attention.

'Ouch! Yes, I'm sure. It goes out mad early, but at eight o'clock it will definitely be fully out. It starts to come in again at about nine.'

The vibration in Gerard's chest woke Fat up. He stretched and yawned, and then slithered out under Gerard's elbow and disappeared under the bed.

'Eight o'clock!' Elizabeth was appalled. 'Do you mean eight o'clock *a.m.*? Like, in the *morning*?'

Gerard nodded.

'Ye gods and little fishes!' exclaimed Elizabeth, who was re-reading *Little Women*. 'It's supposed to be the holiers!'

'Come on, Liz,' said Beverley. 'We are intrepid explorers, remember?'

'What does "interpid" mean?' asked Gerard innocently.

But nobody bothered to answer him. People often didn't bother to answer Gerard, he noticed. He crawled under Elizabeth's bed, after Fat, and he lay there for a while, listening to the mattress-dulled hum of the girls' voices and looking at their ankles moving restlessly under the straggly brown fringes of the bed-spread. Then he sneezed – it was dusty under there – and rolled out on the other side, gathering Fat in his arms as he did so. His shirt crackled with static from contact with the brown nylon carpet, and Fat's fur stood up on end like a yard brush.

Elizabeth turned to look at her cousin, struggling up from his knees, his arms full of cat.

'You've got fluff in your hair,' she remarked. 'And so has that filthy cat of yours. And you shouldn't be crawling around under beds. I'm sure dust isn't good for you.'

Gerard said nothing. He found that was the best policy with these girls. That way, they didn't notice you so much, and they left you alone. He'd see how sprightly Elizabeth would be feeling at eight o'clock the next morning. Ha!

Chapter 3

THAT KEVIN

ELIZABETH WAS NONE TOO SPRIGHTLY at eight in the morning. She never was before breakfast.

'I still think we should have *said*.' Her voice had taken on its whiniest tone, partly because her feet were wet, and she hated having wet feet. It was a damp morning with no atmosphere, not the way dawn is supposed to be. Not that it was dawn any longer. That had happened while they were still deep asleep. But it felt like dawn. The beach was cold and deserted, the shop was firmly shuttered, all the holiday houses still had their hands over their eyes. Only the seagulls were awake.

'You're *supposed* to *say*,' she whinged on, 'you're supposed to say when you're going on a long walk. You're supposed to make sure somebody knows you've gone, and what time you're expected back, so they can send army helicopters after you if you're not home in time for your tea.' Elizabeth was not one for missing her tea, if it was at all avoidable.

'Oh, shut up, Elizabeth,' said Beverley. 'I did say, I keep telling you. It's just that adults don't listen properly when you tell them stuff. I said you and I and Gerard were going on a picnic, and "That's nice," was all she said. So it's her lookout if she doesn't know where we are. Anyway, you said so too. I heard you telling *your* mother we were going on a hike today.'

'Yes, but we never said we'd be gone before they all woke up. We didn't say anything about sneaking out at the crack of dawn without our cornflakes.'

'It's not the crack of dawn,' Beverley pointed out with her usual maddening pedantry. 'In some countries, people would be in their offices by now.'

'You're supposed to ring the coastguard, or someone like that, and tell them how long you'll be gone for.'

'That's only for seagoing vessels,' said Beverley. 'There's no such protocol for picnics on islands.'

Elizabeth didn't know what a protocol was, but she knew Beverley was wrong, and she also knew Beverley deliberately used hard words like 'protocol' just to get the better of Elizabeth. But she wouldn't ask her what it meant – that would only give her ammunition.

Gerard toiled away silently, doggedly pulling each foot out of the wet sand with a gentle plop at every step. Fat had put his arms around Gerard's neck, in a rare gesture of affection that meant he was doing his best to co-operate, but the result was that Gerard couldn't really see where he was going. The cat's lolling head got in the way. But he dared not hurt Fat's feelings, not after all that had happened with the Volvo and the woollen lead and everything.

They had just left the soft sand of the beach, with its tattered carpeting of dried-up, fly-infested seaweed above the tideline, had crossed the brief band of rippled firmer sand closer to the sea, and had ventured onto the wet and sloppy causeway to the island. The tide was well out and the air was acrid with salt and iodine. It would have been easier to walk if they could have taken their runners off, but it was too cold still for this, even though the sun had been up for hours, and the day was only a bit misty.

Elizabeth's runners leaked. She'd forgotten how badly. Her socks clung damply to her toes, and sand lodged between them uncomfortably. She wished she hadn't agreed to come on this silly outing. It was ridiculous sneaking out of the house like a thief. Why did she agree to things old Bossy-Boots Beverley suggested? She'd only known her for three days.

Elizabeth wished for the third or fourth time she'd left a reassuring note for her parents. Why hadn't she said something more explicit to them yesterday? Just because Beverley didn't get on with her parents was no reason for Elizabeth to behave badly to hers. Elizabeth's parents were cool. She should have told them. She shouldn't have let the idea of an adventure silence her.

'I think I'll go back and leave them a note,' she said with sudden decisiveness, stopping in her tracks.

'It's too late now,' said Beverley. 'We have to get to the island before the tide changes.'

'Oh lord! But I'll only be ten minutes.'

The house the Ryans were renting was almost right on the beach, closer than Beverley's family's cottage.

Beverley sighed. 'Well, don't blame me if you get left behind,' she warned Elizabeth, who had already turned back.

Coming down the beach towards them was a figure dressed in black. Only Elizabeth could see him because the others were facing in the opposite direction. She stood still for a moment, settled the garden flares against one shoulder and screwed up her eyes to see if she could make out who it was.

'It's that Kevin from the shop!' she called over her shoulder to the others. 'He's coming after us.'

'Oh blast!' said Beverley, turning around. 'What does *he* want? Pretend we haven't seen him. Come on, face the other way and ignore him.'

'But I'm going back to the house.'

'Oh please, Elizabeth. Let's not get *involved* with him.'

Elizabeth hesitated. Then: 'It's too late. He's seen me looking at him. He's waving.'

Spontaneously she raised her free arm and waved it in a long arc.

'Stoppit, Elizabeth!' exclaimed Beverley.

'I'm only being friendly. He's nice.'

Elizabeth waved again.

Kevin was striding along. The dry sand didn't seem to impede his progress as it had theirs. Perhaps local people had developed a method for beach-walking, Elizabeth thought. Maybe they were able to spread their toes in a certain way, so that they worked like snowshoes, allowing them to glide swiftly over the sand. Perhaps their toes were webbed, even. Kevin had reached the hard, compacted sand at the waterline now.

'Hallo-o-o!' he called, picking up into a trot now that he was on a firm surface.

'Hiya!' called Elizabeth, with a beam. She'd forgotten all about going home.

In no time, Kevin was on the waterlogged stretch of sand that led to the island. Elizabeth stood and waited for him to catch up.

Even Kevin had some difficulty with this part of the sand. He stopped for a moment to hitch up his jeans at the knees and came plashing along more slowly to join Elizabeth, who still stood with her back to the island, watching him.

When he reached her, Kevin stopped and lifted one foot

gingerly into the air, and reached out to roll up the bottom of his jeans. Then he lowered that foot, and did the same with the other, jutting his elbows out to balance himself. He looked like some demented black heron.

'Hi,' said Elizabeth again. 'We're going out to Lady Island. We have a picnic.'

She turned to point out her companions, but Beverley and Gerard were away ahead of them now, two bright rucksacks with legs, in the distance.

'Lady Island?' said Kevin, sounding a bit surprised. 'Oh! A picnic! Well, well.'

Elizabeth couldn't for the life of her see what Beverley had against this lad. He was perfectly pleasant, though he seemed a bit startled at the idea of taking a picnic out to the island.

'Yep.' Elizabeth nodded in the direction of the island, green and hazy and large from this perspective.

Kevin was silent. He thrust his hands into his pockets, hunched his shoulders and buried his chin in his neck.

'It's not haunted or anything, is it?' asked Elizabeth, peering into Kevin's face.

'Well ...' said Kevin. He dug his heels into the sand and swivelled on them. 'Arrah, no, no,' he went on, as if he were trying to sound more decisive than he really felt. 'No. I don't think you could call it haunted,' he said slowly.

'And it wouldn't be trespassing, would it?'

'How do you mean, like, trespassing?'

'I mean, does it belong to someone? Someone with a Doberman, for example?'

'Doberman?' Kevin looked puzzled. 'No. I never heard tell of a dog.'

28

'Good,' said Elizabeth, glad that that had been cleared up. 'Are you going to come with us so?'

'Me? Oh! But sure, I'm not ...'

And he stopped. He'd been going to say he wasn't one of them, but he thought maybe that sounded a bit rude, or maybe a bit self-pitying.

'Come on, I'm inviting you,' said Elizabeth, picking up what he meant. 'If you like.'

'Yeh, but what about Miss High-an'-Mighty?' Kevin cocked a thumb in the direction of the rucksacks bobbing along ahead of them.

'Bev? Oh, don't mind her. Her bark's worse than her bite – I think.'

'Have ye enough of picnic for us all? I wouldn't want to be eating someone's rations.'

'We have enough for a small army.'

Kevin thought for a moment. He knew Beverley wouldn't want him. She was far too stuck up for the likes of him. But this other girl was nice and friendly. And it would be interesting to see what it was like on the island. The locals always kept well away from there. But there was really no reason to be afraid. She wasn't dangerous or anything – at least he didn't think so. And he had nothing else to do. It was his sister's turn to help in the shop. He'd done the delivery to the pier already, and he had the rest of the day off. It was unusual for him to get a whole day off, so it would be nice to use it properly, instead of just kicking about on the beach and maybe doing a bit of fishing in the afternoon. And anyway, he couldn't really let them off on their own. They might get into some sort of trouble, these Dublin youngsters, all by themselves out there. Really, they'd be much better off if they had him to watch out for them. Because you never knew.

'Right you be, so. I'll come.' Kevin put out his hand for the garden flares. 'I'll carry them yokes for you. Whatever they are.'

Kevin and Elizabeth started to struggle after the others, slithering along the slimy causeway, lurching together and laughing when they bumped into each other, stepping over rivulets cut into the sand by ropes of sucking seawater and over streamers of gleaming wet seaweed, slurping through puddles and pools left behind by the tide, carefully circling around black and slippery rocks.

By the time they reached the far beach, on the island, the tide was already on the turn, and little wavelets were starting to lap around their ankles.

Chapter 4

BREAKFAST ON THE
ISLAND

ELIZABETH AND KEVIN CAME ASHORE splashing and laughing.
They had had to take off their runners for the last few hundred
yards of the journey and tie them around their necks, as the water
was starting to whirl around them in threatening little eddies, as
if a giant bath were being slowly filled by unseen taps. The
bottoms of their jeans were wet, though they tried to keep them
out of the waves. Their runners were hopelessly waterlogged.

Beverley was sitting waiting for them on the tiny island beach,
with a glowering expression on her face, like somebody's mother
when they've been out past their curfew time.

'What's he doing here?' she asked Elizabeth through clenched
teeth, nodding towards Kevin, but not meeting his eyes.

'I – well, I'm – I'm not sure,' spluttered Elizabeth, taken aback
at just how rude Beverley could be. 'What are you doing here,
Kevin?'

'You asked me,' said Kevin simply.

'Oh, so I did!' said Elizabeth with a peal of laughter. 'I invited
him, Beverley,' she added defiantly.

'And what's he going to eat?' Beverley was not amused. It was
her expedition after all. Elizabeth had no business inviting any-

one, least of all that Kevin. 'He seems to have one hand as long as the other, as far as I can see.'

'Oh, give over, Bev. There's loads to eat. What were you doing on the beach, Kevin, at Tranarone, I mean, at this hour of the morning?'

'Oh, em, just walking,' said Kevin evasively, kicking a stone and running a hand through his hair, which lay down again neatly as soon as he'd riffled it.

He must spend a fortune getting it cut, Beverley thought. Really, when you thought about the poverty in the world!

Kevin didn't really want to start explaining about the pier delivery. That would only bring up the whole business of Herself, as the local people called her, and that wouldn't be a good idea, not if Elizabeth was a bit worried about trespassing. There was no harm in her, some people said, but even so, you never knew. Maybe they wouldn't have to meet her. If they were just here for a picnic, well then, they could have it and be home before dinner time and there wouldn't be any problem. Not that it was a problem. Not really.

'Where's Gerard?' Elizabeth asked. 'I think I'm going to have to take these jeans off,' she added, not waiting for Beverley's reply.

'Elizabeth!' Beverley sounded more and more like an outraged parent.

Elizabeth was pulling her jeans down over her knees, revealing a pair of pink-spotted pants.

'What?' asked Elizabeth crossly.

'You can't go around in your *knickers*!'

'Oh, for heaven's sake, Bev, gimme a break! It's only till my jeans dry a bit. Anyway, we're on the beach. People go around half-naked on the beach all the time.'

Beverley jerked her head frantically, warningly, in the direction of Kevin and mouthed at Elizabeth. But Kevin had already moved off up the beach.

Suddenly there was a whoop: 'How'ya, kiddo!' Kevin had spotted Gerard, who was toiling away farther up the beach, gathering driftwood for a fire, with Fat under one arm.

'Here!' said Beverley, diving into her rucksack and producing a pair of striped blue and white shorts. 'Put these on.' And she thrust them hurriedly at Elizabeth. 'Quick!'

'Oh, ta,' said Elizabeth, who was starting to feel the cold. She wriggled quickly into the shorts and started to dig for her sandals in her rucksack.

Kevin and Gerard came back with an offering of wood in various shapes and sizes, most of it reasonably dry.

'Matches?' asked Kevin, starting to arrange the wood into a fire-shaped heap in the lee of a biggish rock.

'Elizabeth has them,' said Beverley, and added spitefully: 'if she hasn't got them wet too.'

'Course I haven't!' Elizabeth's voice was cheery. 'They're wrapped in three separate plastic bags.' She opened her rucksack and started rootling through it again.

Gerard opened his also, and produced an old and holey towel. He shook it out as best he could with one arm, and spread it on the sand. Then he laid Fat on it reverently. Fat immediately stood up, arched his back and pressed his paws down hard into the towel. Because the towel was laid on loose sand, it skidded under this pressure, and landed Fat flat on his stomach. He yowled and lay there disconsolately for a while, clawing ineffectually at the towel.

'Bloody cat!' hissed Beverley, through clenched teeth.

'Blasted animal!' Elizabeth agreed, still scarching for the matches.

Their eyes met in a complicity of disapproval. Gerard swallowed hard and pretended not to mind. Very gingerly, Fat pulled his legs in, one at a time, folding them up like telescopic aerials. Then he curled himself into a doughnut, tucking his ears well down under his haunches, and went haughtily to sleep. Kevin put out a tentative hand and stroked Fat's fur. Gerard shot him a grateful look. Kevin smiled back at him.

'Here they are!' Elizabeth waved a lumpy plastic-bag parcel. 'And the firelighters!'

'You brought firelighters?' Beverley was irritated that she hadn't thought of them. 'You should have carried them separately from the matches, though. I'm sure it's dangerous.'

Elizabeth sighed. 'Beverley, the firelighters were in a separate plastic bag inside the other one. They weren't even touching. It wasn't dangerous. Now, will you kindly get off my back? You're worse than a teacher!'

Elizabeth pitched two soft white blocks, reeking of petrol, in Kevin's direction. He caught them deftly, set them in nooks in the woodpile and turned to her for the matches. These she threw also. In a moment, the steady flames at the corners of the firelighters has started to stretch up and lick hopefully at the wood.

'What about breakfast?' said Elizabeth, arranging her jeans on a rock near the fire, wet trouser cuffs laid out at an angle to the heat. 'I'm starving.' She propped her runners up against the rock too.

Beverley started to unpack her rucksack slowly, still sulking a bit after the way Elizabeth had spoken to her. But as she pulled food item after food item out of the rucksack, she began to cheer up. 'We'll need the frying pan first, Gerard, and then the kettle.'

'Yes, Beverley, oh yes!'

Gerard leapt up and started to unpack his rucksack too. 'One frying pan coming up. Do you need a knife?'

'Yes.'

'Sharp?'

'Obviously.'

Gerard reddened and handed Beverley a black-handled knife, carefully pointing the handle towards her, as his mother had taught him.

'And a plate, please.'

Gerard handed Beverley an enamel plate. Beverley hung a string of sausages from one hand and started to separate them with quick thrusts of the knife. She laid them in a heap, like grotesque and floppy dismembered fingers, on the plate. Then she pushed them aside and started to slice the black pudding in the space she had cleared. She liked being efficient and getting on with things.

'What are you going to fry them in?' asked Kevin, interested.

'The pan,' Beverley replied with pointed briefness.

'No, I mean, butter or oil or lard, or what?'

'Uh-oh!' said Beverley.

'Did we forget something?' asked Gerard anxiously, as if it had been his responsibility to pack the food.

'It doesn't matter,' snapped Beverley, pricking the sausages savagely with the point of her knife. 'The sausages will cook in their own fat. And there'll still be enough to cook the pudding and rashers in.'

She placed the pan on the fire and let it heat through. Then she threw the sausages into it, higgledy-piggledy, and pushed them around with the knife. The sausages started to cook with a fierce black stench, not the spicy-sweet inviting smell cooking sausages are supposed to produce. And there was no inviting sizzle either. The sudden heat seemed to have sealed up the holes that Beverley had slashed in them, and the expected juices didn't flow. This wasn't working out the way Beverley had planned it. Irritably, she poked at them, trying to pierce their thickening skins again, but they spat back at her uncooperatively. Suddenly they all split right down the centre, with a series of hissing pops, and fat started to race around the pan in hopping droplets. Into this seething lakelet, Beverley bounced the pudding slices, which immediately shrivelled and hardened.

While they cooked, Beverley cleaned her plate with sand and as soon as she judged everything was ready, she tipped the contents of the pan back onto the plate. Then she deftly slid her knife between the rasher layers, to separate them, and laid them out, four long pink strips, on the pan, in the blackened juices of the sausages.

Meanwhile, Elizabeth and Gerard had taken out the crockery and cutlery and started to divide the breakfast among the four of them. They sat on the sand and ate sausages and pudding, followed by fried bread and rashers.

'How can something be both burnt and raw at the same time?' asked Gerard, regarding a thing on the tip of his fork with puzzled interest.

Beverley glared at him. 'What do you mean, burnt? What do you mean, raw?'

'Like this,' said Gerard, holding out a charred piece of pudding with a purplish centre, still not realising that the question he posed as a scientific puzzle was being understood as a criticism of the cook.

'It's supposed to look like that,' snapped Beverley. '*Sanglant*, you call it. That's the way they do it in expensive restaurants.'

Kevin was kneeling at the fire, making tea, using the fresh water the others had hauled over in a gallon container. He sat back on his heels at this point with the kettle in his hand and threw his head right back, as if he were doing some elaborate yoga position. '*Sanglant*!' he spluttered. His adam's apple rippled alarmingly as he roared with laughter. 'That's a good one!' The longest parts of his hair fell back between his black leather shoulder blades and almost touched the soles of his bare feet. When he straightened up, his hair sat back again on his head, like a well-fitting cap.

Beverley couldn't help admiring this, though she didn't appreciate being laughed at. She wondered if she could get her own hair cut like that. Absently, she put her hand to her frizzy mop and ran disappointed fingers through it, snagging at knots and tangles at every point.

Gerard longed to apologise for the remark about the burnt pudding, but he didn't know how to, without making it worse, so he just chewed miserably.

'Did ye bring a taypot?' asked Kevin, exaggerating his local accent. 'Or would that be a posh enough class of a thing for this high-class restaurant? Maybe it's a samovar you like your tay made in, Madam?'

Beverley blushed, but she couldn't help being impressed that he knew a word like samovar. 'We didn't bring a teapot,' she said sullenly. 'We tried to keep the load light. Make it in the kettle.'

'Right so,' said Kevin cheerfully, dropping two teabags into the bubbling kettle.

The tea tasted unaccountably of sausages, but nobody, not even Gerard, mentioned this.

After they'd all put milk in their tea, Elizabeth produced a clothes peg and carefully pegged the carton closed, to keep the sand out of it. Beverley watched jealously. Where did Elizabeth get such a sensible idea from? It wasn't as though she was clever or anything.

The beach was just beginning to warm up as they finished their meal. The bay had filled completely with water by now, like a shallow soup bowl, and it was starting to glimmer, just faintly.

'I think it's going to be a good day,' said Elizabeth, looking encouragingly at the sun as it peered out hesitantly from the mist. 'Someone must have broken the news to them up there that it's summer.'

She sat back against the breakfast rock, her legs stretched out full length in front of her and took a long, satisfied, luke-warm sip of milky, sausagey tea. 'Bless you!' she said suddenly, without thinking.

'What?' asked Beverley.

'I just said "Bless you!"'

'That's what I thought you said, but why? I didn't do anything particularly nice, did I?'

'No, but you sneezed, didn't you? I always say "Bless you!" when someone sneezes. It's so the devil doesn't come and take them away.'

'But I didn't sneeze,' Beverley insisted.

Both girls looked accusingly at Gerard, who was always coughing and wheezing and making gurgling noises.

'It wasn't me,' said Gerard. 'I don't sneeze – much. I cough.'

Everyone looked at Kevin.

Kevin looked slowly around, eyeing the beach, the sea, the rocks, and the sand-dunes behind them. Nothing moved, except for the waves rushing up the beach and being sucked back down again.

'I think it must have been yer man the cat,' he said at last. 'Maybe he's what-d'ye-call it – allergic, that's it – maybe he's allergic to sand.'

But he wondered. He just wondered.

Chapter 5

ELIZABETH'S TALE

AFTER THEY'D HAD THEIR BREAKFAST, the children felt drowsy. They'd been up early (for the holidays) and they'd had a long walk in the sea air followed by hot food and tea.

'Let's have a little rest,' suggested Elizabeth, 'before we go exploring the island. Let's just sit here for a bit and have another cup of tea.'

'Hmm,' said Beverley, 'and what about the washing-up?'

'Oh, we can do that later,' said Elizabeth. 'Pass us a biscuit, Bev.' And she leant back against her rock and closed her eyes and pointed her face up to catch the weak heat of the morning sun.

Then suddenly she said in a strange voice, still with her eyes closed: 'Once there were four children, two boys and two girls.'

'Wha-at?' asked Beverley, fishing a packet of only slightly squashed Bourbon Creams out of the larder rucksack and passing them around. 'What are you wittering about, Elizabeth? Talk sense, can't you?'

'I'm telling a story,' said Elizabeth in her strange, faraway voice, like someone who was hypnotised or entranced. 'Why don't you just listen?'

'A story! Good grief, Elizabeth, what do you think this is? Jackanory time at playschool? Now, listen, I think we should just wash up and get ready to go. We haven't got all day, you know.'

Beverley was beginning to be sorry she'd got all these others involved in her little expedition. She should just have come on her own and had a proper explore all by herself and done it her own way. Between Gerard with his irritating breathing and his mangy cat and that awful Kevin with the hair muscling in without so much as a by-your-leave and now Elizabeth going all dreamy and starting to spout nonsense, she was thoroughly fed up with the lot of them. They deserved each other. Maybe she could just leave them here on the beach and head off on her own.

'But we *have* got all day, Beverley,' said Gerard daringly. He wanted to hear what Elizabeth had to say. 'Is it a story about us, Elizabeth?'

Elizabeth opened her eyes to look at him and was just about to answer when Beverley cut in again: 'Oh, shut up, you little brat, Gerard. And as for you, Elizabeth, you've got the child all confused with your stupid storytelling.' Really, she thought, Elizabeth was as big a baby as Gerard was.

'Don't call me a child, Beverley,' said Gerard stoutly. 'I mean,' he corrected himself, as he liked to be accurate, 'I *am* a child, I know, but you make it sound like an insult.'

'Yeh, you do,' Kevin chipped in unexpectedly. 'There's no need to be so rough on him, Beverley. He's only a young lad.'

Beverley was furious. Who did this local boy, this – this – this *yobbo* think he was, telling *her* how to behave? And on *her* expedition. She hadn't even invited him.

'Oh shut up you too, Kevin Mulrooney,' she snapped at him. 'You're nothing but – but – but a shopkeeper's son and a culchie to boot!'

Elizabeth drew in her breath sharply. Gerard looked as if he would burst into tears.

'There's nothing wrong with having a shop,' Kevin snapped back, 'or with being a culchie either. Better than a snotty-nosed townie any day, anyways.' (He pronounced it anny-ways, to Beverley's deep disgust.)

'And if the culchies are so terrible,' he went on, before Beverley could snap back again, 'why do you come down here on your holidays, you stuck-up snob, you? Is it a thing that ye can't get enough air up there in Dublin or what? All traffic and dirt and crime and people running around with their mobile phones, trying to look important, that's all Dublin is. And then ye come down here for the summer and look down yeer pointy little noses at us and ask us have we no *posta* or *gorr*-lick and "whot taim does the *Gawrdian* come in?" and "is there nowhere around here we con get a deecent cup of express-oah?" Ah, ye make me sick, lettin' on to be English or French or whatever it is, and afraid to be seen dead puttin' red sauce on yeer chips.'

Gerard started to giggle nervously.

Beverley was bright red. She didn't know how to respond to this attack, partly because, if she were quite honest, she recognised herself in what Kevin had said. She had asked him that very question about the *Guardian* the other day, and she'd heard her mother giving out about not being able to get a cup of *espresso* in the pub.

'There's no need to be so bloody rude,' she mumbled, unconsciously feeling her nose to see if it was pointy. 'And that goes for you too, Specky,' she added viciously to Gerard.

Gerard blushed deeply and pushed his glasses up his nose with an anxious little movement.

'I'm sorry,' said Kevin gruffly. 'But you were rude to me first, and there's no need to take it out on the young lad either. And it's a nice shop, so it is.'

'It's a grand shop,' said Elizabeth brightly, eager to smooth over this little unpleasantness. 'And it's true, Beverley, you were rude to him first.' She didn't say anything about how rude Beverley'd been to Gerard. It seemed being rude to him was acceptable.

'Well, I didn't ask him to come,' said Beverley sulkily. 'Don't you start taking his side.'

'Look, would the pair of you give it over and act your ages?' Elizabeth pleaded. 'And can I just get on with this story?'

Beverley simmered, but she didn't argue any more. She knew she'd been horrible to Kevin, but she couldn't bring herself to apologise as he had done. Better let Elizabeth's intervention do instead. She sniffed, and shrugged her shoulders. And anyway her nose wasn't pointy, she knew that.

'One day,' Elizabeth continued, with her eyes closed again, 'they went for a walk in the woods. And as they went along, they ate the berries that they found there.'

Beverley couldn't help snorting at this, and she started to wash up the breakfast things noisily in protest, but she didn't raise any more objections to Elizabeth's story. She stopped for a moment to thrust a tea-towel at Kevin. He might as well make himself useful, now that they were stuck with him. He wiped away agreeably enough, but Beverley could see his mind wasn't on the job. He was listening to Elizabeth and her precious story.

'Not because they were hungry,' said Elizabeth, raising her voice above the clattering of the dishes, 'but because the berries were so delicious. They looked just like really ripe blackberries, except that they were as big as plums, and they tasted like really ripe blackberries too. At least, that's what one of the children

43

thought. Another of them thought they tasted like enormous cherries, and another thought they tasted like honey-sweet melons. In fact, the berries were enchanted berries, and they tasted of whatever it was you most enjoyed eating. For some people they even tasted like fish and chips. For this reason, the children called them wishberries.'

'Wishberries!' Gerard breathed. 'Did you hear that, Fat? Wish-berries.'

'Mmm,' said Kevin appreciatively, but quietly, so as not to offend Beverley more than was really necessary.

'Humph!' said Beverley.

'Now, what the children didn't know was that the wishberries were enchanted in another way also. Pigberries they were called by the locals, because it was said that if you ate them you would turn into a pig.'

Elizabeth paused for effect.

'Go *on*, Elizabeth, *did* they turn into pigs?' asked Gerard. Beverley was moving the dishes more quietly now.

'Well, that was the funny thing, you see,' said Elizabeth. 'They did and they didn't.'

'Woo-oo!' said Gerard, his eyes wide.

'They did and they didn't?' repeated Beverley, who didn't like ambiguity. 'What's that supposed to mean?'

'That is to say,' said Elizabeth carefully, her audience silent now with anticipation, 'one of them turned into a pig, one of the older ones, a girl, but the others didn't.'

'Why?' asked Gerard.

'Because,' said Elizabeth, 'because they were all turning into other things.'

'Gosh!' whispered Gerard.

44

'You see, pigberries was not quite an accurate name. It is true that a local person had turned into a pig after eating the berries, but the way the berries worked was like this: you turned into whatever animal you most resembled. This particular person had happened to turn into a pig and so they were called pigberries.

'The eldest, a boy, he turned into a very tall and beautiful black heron, with very long spindly legs and a long, black neck and wonderful glowing coal-black feathers. When he wanted to talk to his brothers and sisters, he had to duck down very carefully so that he didn't catch his neck in the branches of the trees, as he was very tall.'

'You never said they were brothers and sisters,' interrupted Beverley. She seemed to have stopped washing up, though she'd only got halfway through.

'Did I not?' said Elizabeth with a frown. 'Well, they were.'

'That's nice,' said Gerard wistfully. 'Three brothers and sisters must be nice.'

'Then, as i said,' Elizabeth went on, 'the next, a girl, she turned into a pig, a small, dainty sort of a pig with an extremely curly tail and dumpy, stumpy little legs which she had to move very quickly in order to make any kind of progress over the ground at all.

'And the other girl, she became a fawn, swift as the wind and lithe as a lath.'

'Lithe as a *lath*?' exclaimed Beverley. 'You can't say that! Laths aren't lithe.'

Elizabeth considered for a moment. 'Poetic licence,' she said at last. 'Anyway, they made all their laths of willow in that country, you know, which is very springy.'

'Very springy!' repeated Beverley scornfully, far from satisfied with this explanation.

'What about the last one, the other boy?' Gerard asked.

'Oh yes, well, he turned into a furry little hamster, a nice chocolate-brown one, a bit on the slim side for a hamster, but very warm and comforting to hold.

'But the strange thing was, the children didn't know that they had changed into these creatures at all. The heron went stepping on through the woods, carefully lowering his head from time to time to talk to the piglet and the piglet went trotting along as fast as her trotters would carry her and still not getting very far, and the fawn went leaping and sailing through the air, her pretty little hooves barely skimming the ground, and the poor little hamster went snuffling along at a great rate, wearing his little heart out with the effort of keeping up with the others. He would make a quick scuttling movement and fly away ahead, but then he would be worn out and have to stop for a rest, his bright eyes darting around in case there might be an owl on the prowl, though it was broad daylight, and by the time he had got his breath back the others would have passed him out.

'And so they went on through the woods, leaping and scuttling and trotting and stalking, still eating pigberries whenever they felt like it and talking to each other whenever they all managed to be in the same place at the same time.

'They were all having a grand time, but after a while, whether it was all the trotting and scuttling and so on, or what, they all began to feel very tired, and just as they were looking around for somewhere nice and mossy where they could settle down for a rest, something awful happened. The merry little fawn was skimming along lithely as usual when suddenly she was caught in a horrible trap. It just grabbed her by the hoof and dug its horrible teeth into her.

'Well, that was the end of the little fawn's leaping and bounding. She was well and truly grounded now – in fact she could hardly move at all without inflicting dreadful pain on herself.

'The heron was the first to reach her. He ducked his head gracefully down through the greenery and examined the raw, bleeding wound, with the nasty metal teeth of the trap still embedded in it.

'Then up trotted the pig, anxiously snuffling the earth and gently nudging her sister with her soft, pink snout.

'And finally the hamster came scooting along in a flurry of fallen leaves and with his tail lashing from side to side like a rudder. He curled up behind the fawn's ear and whispered comforting whistles to cheer her up.

'The animal-children were all wondering what to do when the heron raised his glorious neck to give it a rest from ducking down and spotted, away among the trees, the sweetest little gingerbread house you ever saw.'

'Uh-oh!' said Gerard softly.

'Yes,' said Elizabeth, 'precisely. Well, it had a liquorice-allsort chimney, you know, the black cylinder one with the white stuff in the middle.'

'My favourite,' breathed Gerard.

'Yes, that one, and it had a little puff of candy floss coming out of it.'

'Oh my, for smoke,' said Gerard, enchanted.

'Yes, for smoke. And the roof was thatched with boudoir biscuits. The walls were slabs of golden gingerbread, and the window-panes were made of slices of glacier mints.'

'What about the door?' asked Gerard.

'A Jersey Cream biscuit.'

'Edinburgh rock for the fence?'

'Is that the chalky kind?'

'Yes, sort of.'

'Well that's it then,' said Elizabeth.

'What about the fawn?' asked Beverley, who felt the story was getting diverted a bit by the building of this house.

'Oh yes, the fawn. Well, the heron and the pig said they would go to the house for help.'

'That's what I was afraid of,' said Beverley.

'Why?' asked Kevin.

'Well,' said Beverley, hardly noticing that she was conversing with Kevin, 'because of the witch.'

'Oh, the witch,' said Kevin. 'Wait a minute, what witch?'

'The one in the gingerbread house.'

'But they weren't – hey, hang on there now a minute! Whose story is this anyway? How do you know what's going to happen in Elizabeth's story?'

'She doesn't know. She's wrong,' said Elizabeth. 'Will everyone please stop talking and let me get on with it?'

'Sorry,' said Kevin and Beverley together.

'Well, when they got to the house, there was the grandmother sitting up in bed.'

'The witch,' Beverley mouthed.

Elizabeth saw what she was saying.

'No, the wolf,' she said triumphantly, 'with a striped nightcap on to cover his long ears and a long nightshirt on to cover his hairy body.

'As soon as the grandmother, I mean the wolf, saw the heron bobbing in at his front door, he started to dribble with excitement at the thought of stuffed heron roasted with rosemary sprigs and glazed potatoes.

'And when he looked down at the heron's ankles and saw a plump little piglet there, he drooled even more at the thought of crackling and sage stuffing and apple sauce.

'But as soon as the heron, who was tall and had a better view of the world, saw the wolf in grandmother's clothing sitting up in bed, he knew the danger they were all in. He knew that they would have to think of a way of getting the better of the wolf. So he stepped up to the edge of the bed and bent his long black neck down and whispered in the wolf-grandmother's ear: "Woodcutter alert! You'd better clear out of here quick. Go out the back door and head for the hills. And whatever you do, don't look back, or you'll be turned into a pigberry tree." That was why there were so many pigberry trees around – a lot of curious wolves they were really.

'"Woodcutters!" yelped the wolf, leaping out of bed and tearing the night-clothes off. "How many?"

'"Seven," said the heron, "and their seven husbands too. Quick now!"

'But the last sentence never reached the wolf's ears, for he was off out the back door, leaving it hanging on its liquorice bootlace hinges, and over the hills and far away, and he never came back to the gingerbread cottage from that day to this, and he may be still running for all I know.

'So then the heron and the piglet had a good snoop around the little house, helping themselves to candy door handles or clove rock bath taps as they pleased – which grew back again straight away – and before long they had found the wolf's magic medicine chest under the bed.

'It was full of unctions and oils and salves and unguents and balms and, and, and – liniments and poultices, and – lotions and potions, and tablets and pills, and draughts and powders and tisanes of all sorts, and there was also a Manual of Cures and Spells, conveniently printed with orange-fizz ink on rice paper.

'It didn't take them long to find what they needed – a spell for opening traps and an ointment for broken skin. So they tore the page with the spell out of the book, and the piglet took the phial of ointment carefully in her mouth, and off they went back to the hamster and the fawn.

'Their brother and sister were delighted to see them. They had seen the wolf heading for the hills at the speed of light, and they were hoping furiously that the heron and the piglet weren't already inside his inside.

'In a twinkling, the heron had said the spell for opening traps, and as if by magic – oh, no, it *was* actually magic – the trap opened up and released the fawn's injured leg. To celebrate this, the heron ate the spell. It tasted of nothing very much with orange.

'Meanwhile, the piglet smeared the special ointment on the fawn's wound and before their very eyes it completely healed up and left not so much as a scab or a scar.'

'Deadly,' breathed Gerard.

'And with that, the fawn leapt into the air with a wild bound, and the piglet fell in behind at a respectable trot and the heron stepped along in their wake. The poor little hamster landed in a clump, having fallen right off his perch when the fawn jumped up, and with a sigh he gathered his strength and put all his energy into catching up with the others.'

Elizabeth stopped.

'Did they not turn back into children?' asked Gerard, not wanting the story to end.

'No.'

'Why not?'

'No handsome frogs to kiss them, I suppose,' said Elizabeth complacently.

'That was a cool story, even if they didn't turn back into children,' Gerard pronounced.

'Yeh, it was grand, great,' said Kevin good-naturedly.

'Hamsters don't have long tails,' was the best Beverley could manage to say.

'Oh lordy,' said Elizabeth. 'I suppose he might have been a gerbil then. How long is a gerbil's tail, Miss Know-All?'

'Long enough,' said Beverley, grudgingly.

'So he was gerbil then, all right?'

'All right,' said Beverley, 'all right, all right.' And she went back to sloshing the dishes around in the washing-up bucket.

Chapter 6

INTREPIDLY INTO THE
INTERIOR

AFTER THE STORY, THE OTHERS HELPED BEVERLEY to clear away the rest of the breakfast things, and pack everything neatly in the rucksacks. Then they were ready to explore the island.

'It's not very big,' said Beverley, wiping her hands. 'I think we could cover the whole of it by lunch time. Now, my plan is to make a map. We can write down anything interesting we see and put it in on the map.'

'Oh *boring*!' exclaimed Elizabeth. 'Let's not bother with a map. Let's just explore for the *fun* of it.'

Beverley felt a wave of irritation wash over her, making her scalp prickle and her nose twitch. Whose expedition did Elizabeth think this was? But she decided not to make an issue of it. Generously, she ignored Elizabeth's childishness and asked, by way of changing the subject: 'Should we take a picnic lunch with us, or plan to be back here for lunch?'

Lunch! thought Kevin. How long were they planning to spend on the island, then? He was hoping they'd all have got tired of this exploring game long before lunch. Maybe it wasn't such a good idea to have come after all. Still, he couldn't have let them off on their own. Goodness knows what might have happened. He started to calculate times in his head. This was the woman's grocery day. That meant she'd have to row to the mainland to pick up the box he'd left on the pier for her earlier that morning. Sometimes she took the opportunity to do a bit of business in the village, but she didn't really like to be seen, so most days she just picked up the box and rowed straight back to the island. She liked to be gone before the village woke up properly. Assuming she stuck to that pattern today, she'd be bound to be back soon, within an hour at most. They should clear off before the tide was fully in.

'Oh, a picnic, definitely,' said Elizabeth, starting to open up plastic bags and polythene boxes again. 'We have to be prepared for all contingencies.'

What are contingencies? Gerard wanted to ask, but he thought the better of it.

'You never know what might happen between now and lunch,' Elizabeth went on. 'There could be *anything* in the interior.' It gave her a little frisson of delicious horror just to say that.

'The *interior*?' gasped Kevin.

Beverley could see that he had not read the right island books *at all*.

But Kevin was still silently calculating. How much did Beverley know? How much did any of them know? Should he say something, or would it be better just to keep quiet? There was no point in frightening them, after all. And anyway, there wasn't really anything to be frightened of. Or was there? People were probably exaggerating.

'If we're back in time for lunch,' Elizabeth was going on, 'well and good, and I think we should aim to be here for oneish, but we're going to need rations too, just in case.'

Elizabeth was really getting into the spirit of this exploration

53

business. She seemed to have set aside her doubts about the whole idea. She laid out a row of sliced pan slices on a rock and deftly placed ham and luncheon meat slices on every second one. Then she zipped along the row again, tipping the uncovered slices on top of the covered slices, to make rather boring, unbuttered sandwiches. She gathered the sandwiches into piles and sliced them with sharp swoops of the knife.

'There!' she said, laying the neat pink-and-white layers in a lunchbox. 'And we'll have these too.' She picked up the pears and a random selection of fizzy drinks cans and bundled the lot, together with two large bars of chocolate, into a small spare rucksack she'd brought inside her main one.

'Everyone take a warm jumper,' Beverley ordered, before Elizabeth took over this expedition completely. 'And their personal emergency chocolate rations.'

'Emergency!' barked Kevin nervously. 'What emergency?' Maybe they did know about the woman after all. Maybe this was a sort of hunting expedition. That would be *awful*.

'Oh, just any old emergency,' said Beverley complacently, to Kevin's great relief. 'You never know.'

No, thought Kevin. You never did know.

'And you, Elizabeth,' Beverley continued, 'put your jeans back on. And everyone take spare socks, too. Just put them in your pockets. Don't forget the compass, Liz, and the torch and the matches. Oh, and the flares too.'

'Is *that* what these yokes are?' asked Kevin, picking up the barbecue candles.

'Not exactly,' said Elizabeth with a giggle. 'They are Beverley's idea of safety first, *à la* Mount Merrion.'

Beverley glared at her. Mystified, Kevin shouldered the

54

candles. He couldn't see what earthly use they were going to be. These kids definitely had some peculiar ideas. They probably got them from books, he decided.

Gerard picked up Fat, who yawned and blinked, but otherwise didn't protest.

They started the climb away from the sea, wobbling a bit on the large cobbles that lined the top of the beach, demarking it from the start of the land proper. When they stepped onto the short, springy grass, sprinkled with tormentil and small, neat, glossy sheep droppings, for all the world like chocolate raisins, they turned to look back at their abandoned breakfast camp, bright and forlorn, the corner of a plastic bag flapping disconsolately under a stone, already belonging to a life they felt they were shedding as they stepped into the unknown.

'Aha! Orchids!' Beverley sat down with a bump to examine a fleshy specimen and write in her sum copy. The unknown would not remain unknown to her for long. She was here to record it, tame it, prove it held no mystery.

Gerard nuzzled into Fat's side. He felt a slight wheeziness coming on, and he didn't want anyone to notice it. Fat yawned, a fish-flavoured yawn. (He'd had pilchard cat food for breakfast.) Gerard closed his eyes and swallowed the wheezy feeling.

'And prunella – self-heal – this bluey one is, I think.'

But no-one was listening to Beverley, crouched on the yellow-dotted, grassy floor, peering at odd streaks of red and blue. They were surveying the island. Where they stood, above the beach, was quite a high point. Most of the island seemed to be a tangle of rocks and brambles, brackens and heathers, sloping away from them, with here and there a shock of gleaming golden gorse. Off to one side, though, was some attempt at cultivation – the remains of stone-walled fields, what looked like potato ridges, some rather poor-looking pasture. Dividing them from the wilderness was a narrow, flat-bottomed trough that might have been a roadway once, but now it was grassed over and daisies blazed a yellow-eyed trail down its centre.

'We could follow this path,' said Elizabeth, 'or we could cross it and go over the rocks to the other side of the island.'

'I don't want to follow any old trail,' said Beverley's voice, at knee-level. A trail sounded far too tame. 'Let's cross to the other side.'

'Right you be,' said Kevin quickly, relieved that they were keeping off the trail. No prizes for guessing where that led to. They'd really be better keeping right out of her way. No point in looking for trouble. They could have a lovely walk right across the island, and maybe there'd be a nice beach on the other side, and then they could all go home again, and no harm done. Yes, that would be fine.

'No,' said Elizabeth, in her dreamy voice, 'I think I'd rather follow the trail. I bet this island was inhabited once. Otherwise there wouldn't be a trail. We might find the ruins of a church or graveyard or something.'

'I think maybe we should all stick together, Elizabeth,' said Kevin.

'Oh, I hope not,' said Beverley, standing up and waving each leg in turn to shake off the pins-and-needles that had developed in her feet. She meant she hoped there wasn't a church or grave-yard. She didn't want the island – her island – to have signs of human habitation. She wanted it to be wild. She wanted them to be the first people ever to have set foot here. Of course, there was the matter of the trail, but she chose to ignore that.

'Why don't *you* cross the island, Bev, if that's what you want to do,' said Elizabeth, 'and Kevin can go with you if he likes. I'm sure Gerard will come with me along the trail. And we can all meet up again later.'

'No,' said Kevin, with surprising vehemence. 'Let ye not do that at all. I think–'

'I don't think Kevin wants to come with me,' said Beverley quickly. 'Gerard, you'd rather come with me, wouldn't you?' The last thing she wanted was that Kevin coming with her.

'No, that's not what I mean –' Kevin started to explain, but then stopped, not sure how much to say.

Gerard looked up at Beverley – she was a good head and a half taller – over the warm lump that was Fat. 'I'd love to go with you, Beverley,' he said, truthfully.

'There!' said Beverley.

'Only ...' went on Gerard, 'only, I don't think I could manage Fat over that terrain. I think I better stick to the trail.'

'Well, I don't mind going by myself,' said Beverley huffily, avoiding Kevin's eyes, 'if you lot all want to follow the trail.'

'That's not the way it is at all, Beverley,' said Kevin. 'I'm only thinking we'd be better off if we all stayed together. I'll tell you what, why don't we *all* cross the island? Here, I'll take the blessed cat for you, Gerard.'

Beverley fumed silently. There they went again, first Elizabeth, and now that Kevin. Taking over *her* expedition on *her* island. Had they all forgotten that this had been her idea in the first place?

'No!' she said firmly. 'If Elizabeth wants to go by the trail, let her off. And Gerard's right about the stupid cat. You go with them as well, Kevin. I'll be fine on my own.'

Now what was Kevin to do? If Gerard and Elizabeth followed the trail, the chances were they'd meet the island woman. And if Beverley went wandering off on her own across the island, that mightn't be such a great plan either. Should he go with Gerard and Elizabeth and do what he could to head off trouble if they met the island woman, or should he go with Beverley on the principle that none of them should be alone? While he dithered, the others started to make their plans.

'Let's see,' said Elizabeth. 'Who has a watch?'

'I have,' said Gerard.

'So've I,' said Beverley sullenly. 'It's nearly eleven.'

'OK,' said Elizabeth, 'I vote you two – Kevin and Beverley – cross in a straight line and we'll follow the trail around and let's see if our paths cross. If we don't make it by – oh, let's say half-twelve, you can assume that the trail ran out or something has gone wrong. In that case, head back to the beach. And we'll do the same. Here, you'd better take the emergency provisions. You're more likely to get into trouble than we are. We can't go far wrong on the trail.'

'OK,' said Gerard, glad a decision had been made, and he started to pick his way along the trail, coughing quietly, and looking back over his shoulder occasionally to see if Elizabeth was coming too.

'I think we'd be better keeping together,' said Kevin, desperately, looking after Gerard, and then after Beverley, as they set off in different directions.

Elizabeth looked at Kevin, and all her old misgivings about this whole enterprise came flooding back. There was something about this island. She couldn't put her finger on it, but there was. The local people never came here, which was strange to start with.

She'd known before they left the mainland that they shouldn't have come without telling anyone, and she couldn't figure out what had possessed her to keep it all a secret. Anything could happen – they could get hurt or stranded or something – and nobody would know where they were. And then, she'd had a funny feeling since she'd got here. A feeling that they were not alone.

'That's the third time you've said that, Kevin,' she said quietly. 'What's the story?' As she spoke, she gave Gerard (who was looking at her over his shoulder again) an irritable little wave to indicate that he should carry on – she'd be along in a minute.

Kevin shifted his feet about and looked at the ground. 'Story?' he said. 'How do you mean, story?'

'Look, you said yourself there weren't any Dobermans or anything. So that means the wildest thing we're likely to meet is an otter – right?'

'Ye-es.' Kevin hesitated to agree.

'Kevin,' Elizabeth asked, 'does somebody *live* on this island?'

Kevin nodded miserably.

'Oh,' said Elizabeth, and paused for a minute. 'Is it a criminal, or a big wild man with a gun or something?'

'*Not* at all, *not* at all. No, no. Nothing like that at all.'

'Well, then?'

''Tis just – just a woman, really.'

'An ordinary woman?'

'Ordinary? Well now ...'

'Let's say a woman who wouldn't like to be disturbed?'

'Yes, there you have it, now, exactly. You're after putting your finger on it, so you are.' Relief flooded through Kevin. 'She likes to keep herself to herself, you could say.'

Elizabeth thought for a moment. Maybe Kevin was right. Maybe they should all stick together. She turned to call Gerard back, but he was way out of earshot by now. Oh well. What could she do? It was too late now to try to keep the little group together.

'Look,' she said, 'we'll try to keep out of her way, but if we do meet her, we'll be nice and friendly and just say we're on a visit from the mainland. Will that be OK do you think?'

'Yeh, that'll be grand, that's fine,' agreed Kevin, but he didn't sound all that convinced.

Elizabeth shrugged. After all, they'd come to the island for adventure. Now that they'd got here, there was no point in creeping about trying to avoid it.

'Here, give us one of those flare things,' she said. 'We'll send a distress signal if we meet the witch.'

'The witch!' Kevin gasped.

'I was only joking,' said Elizabeth, peering into his face.

'Oh yeh. Heh-heh.' Kevin forced a feeble laugh.

Elizabeth shook her head. She couldn't quite make this Kevin out. Then she smiled at him, and suddenly she was off along the trail, the flare over her shoulder like a rifle.

Kevin watched her marching away from him. She stopped once and turned back to wave at him. He raised his hand in salute. Then he turned and started to climb over the rocks after Beverley.

The rocks were smooth, like huge paving stones with deep cracks in between, from which brambles and flowering plants raised their prickly tentacles and smiling faces, and they shone in the morning sun. The clouds had started a lazy shift across the sky, leaving large splashes of innocent blue, promising a sunny, maybe even a warm day ahead.

Beverley walked ahead of Kevin, even though, not being on a

path, they had plenty of room to walk abreast. Every time Kevin tried to catch her up, Beverley put on a spurt to keep ahead of him. She didn't want to have to make conversation with this person.

They marched along like this for some time, Beverley concentrating on keeping in front, Kevin giving up on the effort to outstrip her. Suddenly a bird flew up in front of Beverley as if out of a crack in the ground and straight up into the air like a helicopter taking off in a flurry of twitters.

'Skylark!' called out Kevin.

'Oh, do you think so?' asked Beverley, turning to him in spite of herself.

'Oh, yeh, I'm positive, so I am. Look how high up it's after rising.' Kevin had his head flung back in a characteristic gesture of his, his hair hanging down between his shoulder blades again.

'I didn't know you knew about birdlife.'

Beverley sat down on a rock, which had lost the cool touch of morning though it wasn't exactly what you could call warm, and took out her sum copy to note the skylark down.

Kevin didn't reply for a moment, just stood there with his head thrown back, watching the bird soaring until it was just a moving speck against the blue of the sky.

'Ah well, I know you think I'm all rock music and motorbikes,' he said, 'but you can't miss knowing about these things when you live in the country, sure they're all around us.'

Beverley bit her lip. She hoped he wasn't going to say something embarrassing.

But he didn't say any more. She closed her notebook, stood up and started to march forward again. This time she slowed her pace, though, so Kevin could fall into step with her.

'The morning time is sort of *clean*, isn't it?' Kevin remarked after a little while, looking sideways at Beverley to see how she was taking this attempt at conversation. 'That's what I always think anyways.'

Beverley knew exactly what he meant, but she didn't know anyone had ever had this thought before, apart from herself. She shot him a surprised look.

Kevin caught the look, like a beach ball, and threw it back at her with a laugh.

'You're right. I *am* into motorbikes. But I'm not a *complete* yobbo all the same.'

'I never said–'

'Arrah, you don't have to say a word at all. If looks could kill, Beverley Wilson, you'd be a mass murderer.'

Beverley laughed, and pulled unconsciously at her corkscrew curls, as if trying to straighten them against the odds.

Chapter 7

ELIZABETH APPEARS TO SWIM
THROUGH A HEDGE

ELIZABETH SOON CAUGHT UP WITH GERARD. He stood back and
let her pass him out – there was no room here for them to walk
side by side – out of a sort of natural politeness that Elizabeth just
took for granted.

As soon as they left the beach area, the trail started to close in,
with greenery invading it from both sides. The path was so narrow,
they kept getting lashed in the face by high-growing bramble
branches that reached out across their path, just at head height.
Everywhere, May blossom was rotting in the hawthorn hedges
with a thick, brown stench, and fuchsia nodded its cardinal-col-
oured heads. There was a low stone wall on the landward side,
overgrown with hedgerow plants most of the time, and what
seemed to be a ditch on the seaward. Insects were about their
buzzy morning business in the undergrowth.

'There have to be sheep,' Elizabeth called over her shoulder,
using the paper-wrapped garden candle as a fencing sword to ward
off a vindictive bramble.

'Why?' asked Gerard, wheezing and puffing along behind her
and stopping to gulp in lungfuls of air every now and then.

'Because of the droppings, nitwit.'

'Oh.' Gerard was used to being insulted by Elizabeth. He didn't even notice any more.

'If there are sheep, there must be a farmer,' she said, half to herself, wondering if that was what the mysterious woman did for a living.

'Why?' asked Gerard again.

'Because sheep are farm animals, of course.'

'Could they not be wild ones?' asked Gerard.

'I suppose so. Maybe.'

'Maa-aa!' said a surprised, sheepy voice, almost in Elizabeth's ear, or so it seemed. She started.

Gerard had heard the sound too, and he was parting the high cow-parsley that lined the trail at this point and waved its fresh-scented creamy heads on a level with their shoulders. Through the gap he created, he could see a sheep, standing half-undressed on a grassy knoll, its coat-tails flapping in the breeze.

'Wow!' said Elizabeth, feeling a bit peculiar. She had the feeling that her talking about sheep had somehow conjured this one up.

'Why is its fur falling off?' asked Gerard.

'Fleece, idiot,' said Elizabeth. 'Because it's summer time. They don't need all that wool in the summer, I suppose.'

'But I thought people shore them,' said Gerard, puzzled.

'Sheared,' said Elizabeth. 'Yes, they do, but if there are no people to do the shearing, then the sheep must shed their wool themselves, I suppose. Maybe there's no farmer, or maybe it's a lazy farmer.'

Elizabeth thought she heard a snorting sound as soon as she'd said this. Surely the sheep couldn't be insulted! What a daft idea! And yet she couldn't get the idea out of her head that it was an offended sort of a sound that she'd heard.

'Are you all right, Gerard?' she asked, remembering his asthma.

'Yes, I'm fine,' he said, though he wasn't really.

Elizabeth looked around to see if someone was listening in to their conversation, somebody who didn't like what they heard. But she couldn't see anyone.

The rational explanation of what happened next was that Gerard, one arm full of cow parsley and breathing carefully, was holding Fat awkwardly and pinched or poked him unintentionally in some way. And yet, Gerard had the impression that someone or something else had provoked or irritated or frightened Fat. Whatever the reason, he leapt with a hiss out of Gerard's arms, cleared the hedge and landed lightly in front of the sheep.

The sheep lowered its long, startled face to examine Fat. Fat arched his back and started a quickstep with the sheep's ankles. The sheep raised its hooves delicately in an effort to avoid the cat, but each time it lowered them, Fat stepped in again between its feet. The sheep started to panic and backed off with a graceless stumbling movement. The cat merely stepped daintily after it, still weaving in and out between its forepaws.

'My God,' said Elizabeth, 'that cat is *worrying* the sheep.'

'Cats don't worry sheep. That's dogs.'

'I know, but if ever I saw a worried sheep, it's that one.'

Certainly the sheep looked intensely concerned.

'Here, I have to rescue the poor creature,' said Elizabeth, thrusting the garden candle at Gerard.

'Oh, I think he's all right. I don't think the sheep will trample him or anything.'

'Janey Mac, Gerard O'Connor! It's the sheep I'm thinking about, not that feline freak!'

Elizabeth put her two arms out as if she were doing the breaststroke, to push the greenery apart, and with a graceful movement she sank into the cool and creamy pool of cow parsley, meadowsweet, elder and woodbine, releasing an intensity of summer-sweet scents as the impact of her body bruised the flowerheads.

Gerard watched her being swallowed up by the undergrowth as if by the waters of a still lake. And then he finally gave way to the asthma attack he'd felt coming on since morning. He sat down hard on the ground and bent over double with the effort of fighting for his breath. He groped in his pocket for his inhaler. Not there! Panic made his breath come even harder. Mustn't panic, he thought, must keep it in control. Just keep breathing, he told himself. He patted his other pocket. There was something there, but it was the wrong shape. It was a chocolate bar, not an inhaler. He must have heard the cry of dismay, followed by a sharply in-drawn breath that was quickly released with a yell of pain, but because he was so taken up with his breathing, for a moment it didn't register with Gerard that this was Elizabeth screaming, yelling, bellowing as she went down.

'Aaaaaaaah!' she roared as her body disappeared. 'There's a flippin' ditch!'

In a moment she came up for air, her arms flailing wildly now.

'I've twisted my ankle, blast and blow and double-blast. Oh! Oh! Help! It hurts!' And down went Elizabeth again, sinking once more into the ditch.

At last Gerard realised that Elizabeth had fallen with a twisting motion onto her ankle, not simply swum gracefully through the hedgerow. With a sudden flash of memory he yanked the hood of his sweatshirt right down over his head and scrabbled madly with his fingers for the hidden pocket inside the hood. Yes, there it was, hard and comforting under his fingers. He rooted it out quickly, yanked the cap off and frantically stuck the inhaler in his mouth, pressing the release button wildly. He drank eagerly, gratefully, at the blessed mist that filled his mouth and immediately his breathing started to come more easily. He took long slow breaths, forcing himself to concentrate on his breathing, though he could hear Elizabeth's yelling as if through a curtain.

As soon as he could breathe easily, he stood up, kicking the garden flare aside, and reached his arm into the spot where he had last seen Elizabeth.

'Here, Liz! Catch hold of my hand!' he yelled.

Elizabeth's arm appeared again out of the sea of green and wavered in the air. Gerard grabbed it by the wrist and heaved, still breathing deeply and evenly. Elizabeth emerged like a lumbering shark caught on a mackerel line. Gerard thought his arm was going to snap at the elbow, and his lungs felt as if they would burst, but he held on for dear life and slowly hauled Elizabeth out of the ditch and back onto the grassy path. In the struggle, Gerard's watch strap snapped, and his watch slithered into the ditch. Blast, he thought briefly. Luckily it had only been a nasty plasticky one he'd got in a pound shop.

Elizabeth lay for a moment gasping for breath, still a bit like a beached shark, and Gerard lay gasping beside her. He opened his inhaler again and took another long in-breath before capping it and tucking it away in his hood. Elizabeth coiled her body into a foetal shape so that she could grab her ankle between her two hands and cradle it. Gently she eased herself into a sitting position, and, still using both hands, she hauled the damaged foot across her other knee and hunched over to examine it.

Both her feet were brown with muck from the floor of the ditch. Carefully, Elizabeth eased off her runners and turned them upside down to drain. Then she peeled off her sopping socks and chafed her sore foot, rocking back and forth with a grieving motion.

Gerard sat miserably beside her and fixed his eyes on her ankle. It was starting to swell already.

'Do you reckon it's broken?' he asked at last.

'No. I can wiggle my toes – just about. But it's badly sprained.'

'Maybe it's just a twist. Maybe it'll be OK in a minute or two.'

'No, it's a sprain all right. I have a weakness in that ankle. Any sort of a twist on it and it puffs up like a balloon. I'm rightly stuck now! And no chance of getting help. It's all Bossy Beverley's fault – she just *had* to keep this whole thing a secret. I don't know what's wrong with her.'

'Now what are we going to do?' asked Gerard, anxiously.

'Apart from a burning desire to drown your cat in the deepest, muckiest stretch of the ditch, I can't suggest anything we might do right this minute.'

'I'm sorry,' whispered Gerard.

Elizabeth looked at his small, worried face and gave him a crooked wink. She'd noticed his desperate sucking at the inhaler. 'It'll be all right,' she said comfortingly. 'Let's just sit and think for a bit.'

They sat and thought. Nothing occurred to them, except that the others had the lunch rations. Neither of them mentioned this gloomy fact, but both of them thought it. And although they'd just had breakfast, they were both suddenly very, very hungry.

Chapter 8

THE OTHER SIDE OF
THE ISLAND

THERE WAS NO BEACH, OR HARDLY ANY, on the other side of the island, just a cliff dropping sheer to the sea. Beverley lay down carefully on her front and poked her head over the edge. Some feet below she could see the greeny water belting itself furiously against the rocks and spewing up masses of white foam like a child in a tantrum foaming vigorously at the mouth. It was hard to believe this was the same sea that they had left less than an hour ago, lapping its way calmly up the beach. It wasn't as though the weather was rough. The sky had cleared now to a pure blue, with just rags of cloud scattered over its surface, and there was only a slight breeze, but still the sea foamed and raged against the cliff.

Beverley looked out to sea. Everything was stiller out there, the mass of water undulating rhythmically under the clear sky. It was only here that the sea boiled and roared. It must have something to do with the shape of the island on this side, jutting out awkwardly into the current and irritating the water by diverting it from the way it wanted to go, so that it lashed out in anger at the rocks and cliffs that trapped it against its will.

As she gazed at it, the sea tilted. Beverley gasped at the clenching sensation this caused deep down in her insides, and closed her eyes. When she opened them again, the sea was just where it should be, not tilting, but still spitting and raging around the rocks. Then suddenly it tilted alarmingly again, and the sensation came back. It was like when an elderly lift arrives in the basement with a jolt and your stomach does a flip inside your abdomen. Again, she closed her eyes against the sensation.

Gingerly, Beverley wriggled backwards, away from the edge. Even though she was lying down, she could feel her knees shaking and her hands were cold and clammy. Her head was light, light as a window, light as a spinning glass sphere. She put her hands up to steady her spinning head, and lay there with her palms pressed against the flaps of her ears so that her head rang with the sound of the waves.

She could hear muffled whoops away above her, like the cries of playing children, fields away. Carefully, she unstopped her ears and tuned in, but without opening her eyes yet. The shaking had stopped. She levered herself onto her elbows. Her stomach was in its rightful place. She sat up altogether. She still felt all right. Her knees were on a nodding acquaintance with each other again. But the whooping was still going on. Yes, it was definitely real, not just a noise in her head.

'Look, Beverley, look!'

The voice was almost down at her ear level now. She could feel the breath of its owner at her neck. She opened her eyes and looked into Kevin's. They were hazel, speckled, shadowy. Well, he might ask how she was feeling, she thought irritably. But he didn't. He didn't know there was anything wrong. He merely repeated: 'Look, look! Turn around and look, can't you!'

'Look at what?' Beverley asked, carefully not looking anywhere near the sea.

'It's seals. Out on the rocks. A whole family of them. Or a tribe maybe. At least a dozen. I bet you've never seen seals this close before.' He didn't add that this was the sort of thing you didn't get to see very often if you lived in the city.

Beverley enclosed her knees in her arms and didn't look around. She could hear the seals barking on the wind.

After a moment, she turned her head seawards with infinite care. From her sitting position she could see the open sea, but not the cliffs and crags and the raging inlet directly below. The ocean rose and fell with a calm rhythm, as if to say, Nothing to be afraid of, everything under control.

Beverley believed the voice of the sea. She found herself adjusting her breathing to its rhythm and the deep, salty breaths she took had a calming effect. She rolled onto her stomach again and started to scan the seascape in front of her for seals. She hadn't seen them when she had looked over the cliff before. They must have been too close to the shore, out of her carefully maintained line of vision. After a moment she spotted them, quite close, as she had expected, ducking and diving, fishing, slithering off the rocks and into the water and swooping underwater. They were very beautiful. Kevin had been right to make her look at them, and no, she had never seen seals so close before, except in the zoo. Even as she watched, one of the seals left the others and started to swim lazily towards the island.

'It's coming ashore!' said Kevin. 'And look, there's another one. And another.' He was jabbing his finger in the air, trying to make Beverley see them as he saw them.

And sure enough, like swallows making a collective decision to migrate, the seals seemed all to have agreed to swim towards the cliffs.

There was a tiny shaly V-shaped beach in a crevice in the cliffs, and it was for here that the seals were aiming. Kevin counted them bellying onto the beach – four, six, seven, nine.

'Beverley,' he said, 'would you like to see them closer? Why don't we climb down to the beach and get a really good look at them? Come on.'

Beverley froze. She dug her fingers into the tough, sparse grass that grew at the cliff's edge, as if to reassure herself that she was on dry land.

'No!' she said. 'No. It's dangerous. No don't, Kevin, please don't,' she pleaded.

'It isn't dangerous at all. Not a bit!' said Kevin. 'Sure it's only a few feet and aren't there loads of footholds? I can see them from here. We'll make it down easy, no bother to us.'

'No, I'm not going,' said Beverley, feeling panic starting up again somewhere in the depths of her insides – her stomach, perhaps, or her pancreas or spleen, somewhere juicy and gurgling and turbulent. She backed away from the cliff again, slithering on her front, and buried her face in the grass, feeling little blades of it tickling her nose, and breathing in the salty, earthy scent of the sandy soil.

'Spoilsport!' said Kevin, already lowering himself over the cliff edge, his back to the sea.

Beverley looked up tentatively and watched Kevin's head disappearing over the edge of the cliff. No, she mustn't look. She closed her eyes again. My God! Suppose he slipped and fell. What would she do? She'd have to rescue him. Panicky feelings started to multiply. She swallowed, as if she could eat her panic, push it down her gullet, into her stomach and digest it. All she could hear were pounding waves, and even though she kept her eyes shut

72

tight she could see endlessly tumbling images of Kevin and herself, herself and Kevin, falling, falling, Kevin and Beverley, Beverley and Kevin, head over heels and heels over head, and all the time falling. She must keep her eyes shut. If she opened them, they might reach the end of their fall and be smashed to pieces on the rocks. As long as she kept her eyes tightly closed, they would just tumble and tumble, rolling images captured against the insides of her eyelids.

'Kevin!' she called out, but there was no reply. Perhaps her cry was lost in the sounds of the sea and the seals barking, or perhaps the wind picked it up and carried it away. 'Kevin!' she called again, louder than before, still not daring to look, but seeing him all the same, hurtling to his death. 'Kevin!' Her throat ached with screaming his name, but there came no reply.

She was going to have to look. Panic fizzed in her head. She crawled forward, to the edge of the cliff, and looked over. Kevin was sprawled against the rocky surface of the cliff.

'Kevin!' she yelled again, the fizzing in her ears so violent now that she could hardly hear her own voice. This time Kevin must have heard, for he raised his head and then he raised an arm to wave at her. My God! He shouldn't let go like that. Was he signalling to her to come and rescue him? Yes, he must be. He must be stuck, pinned to the cliffside.

The secret of conquering vertigo is not to look. She knew that. Swallowing again, she closed her eyes, turned around to face inland and eased her feet over the cliff, her bottom sticking awkwardly out to sea. She found footholds easily, just by kicking with her toes along the face of the cliff until they settled into nooks. She opened her eyes again now, to watch the progress of the top part of her body as she eased herself further down. Her hands left the grassy cliff top and found roots and jutting rocks to grasp. There was a scab on one of her thumbs, where she had cut herself with a breadknife. She concentrated her gaze on that and tried to move automatically, without thinking about what she was doing.

Before long she was level with Kevin. Now what was she going to do? How was she going to effect this rescue? She hadn't thought about this problem – she had been concentrating all her energies on reaching him.

Kevin smiled at her.

'So you're after changing your mind,' he said. 'That's great. It's really dead easy, isn't it?'

'Changing? – rubbish – came to – rescue,' Beverley panted, gripping the cliff-face desperately with her knees.

Kevin's body started to shake alarmingly.

'Don't!' she yelled at him. 'What is it? Oh, stop! You're making me dizzy!'

'Sorry,' Kevin spluttered, but still his body shook. 'But sure what would I need rescuing for, Beverley? It was only waving I was!'

He was laughing. He was laughing at her. She had summoned up her deepest reserves of courage to save him – for nothing. And now he was laughing at her. How dare he!

'Stoppit!' she screeched again. 'Just stop it, you blithering, overgrown, stupid, lunatic, idiotic *boy*!'

'Sorry,' he said again. 'I didn't mean to offend you.'

'You're not offending me. You're terrorising me. You'll fall right back if you laugh like that. You'll lose your grip.'

Beverley didn't know where she found the breath for this absurd conversation, but she had to make him stop.

'No, I won't.' Kevin sobered up. 'We're nearly there, anyways. Come on so.'

With that, Kevin started to slide down the cliff-face, away from Beverley. Sobbing with terror, frustration and indignation, Beverley buried her face in the gritty rock. In a moment she heard a thump. Kevin had landed on the beach he'd been making for.

'Come on, Bev!'

She heard his voice not far below, but she couldn't respond to it. She couldn't move from this spot. All she wanted in the world was not to have to move. She would happily die here, now, transfixed to this cliff, if only she didn't have to move a muscle. If she moved, she would fall into the cauldron of the sea, she knew she would. Anything would be better than moving.

'Easy does it,' Kevin's voice said, closer to her now. He must have started back up the cliff. 'Easy now.'

She felt pressure on her ankle. Frantically, she pulled away, but his pull was stronger than hers and eventually she had to give way to it for fear the struggle would make her lose her grip. As soon as she did, she felt Kevin's hand guiding her foot to a new foothold. Then he tugged the other ankle. This time she went with him. He lodged that foot too in a foothold, lower than the first one. Her body slithered down an inch or two, her hands rasping along the cliff-face. Foothold by foothold he eased her down until she stood gasping and sobbing on the gritty little beach, her arms still akimbo against the rockface and her face pressed to the cliff's unyielding bosom.

Kevin reached up and brought her arms down by her sides. Then he turned her around, to face the sea. She could hear screaming, now, and she felt hot tears on her neck. They had streamed down her face so fast she hadn't felt them on her cheeks.

She could feel them now, though, gathering at the neckline of her T-shirt.

Suddenly, there was a powerful, black, heavy smell and a sensation of dark and warmth and Beverley felt herself being rocked. She could still hear the screaming, but it sounded muffled. She didn't care who or what was screaming. She just wanted the rocking to go on. She wondered for a bit about the smell. She couldn't decide whether she liked it or not. But she liked being rocked. Someone used to rock her like that, she dimly remembered. It must have been her mother. Could it have been? She wouldn't have thought her mother was the rocking type. But perhaps she had been, once.

After a while, the screaming stopped. Now she could hear a thudding sound, like hooves beating steadily along a distant path. She listened to the thudding sound for a moment, and then slowly she pulled away from it, and away from the liquorice-black smell.

When he felt her body relaxing, Kevin loosened his grip on Beverley and opened his black leather, liquorice-smelling jacket to release her head. The thudding sound of his heart beating receded.

Kevin held her wrists still, to steady her. Slowly he loosened his grip on one wrist and dug in his pocket. Then he produced a crumpled tissue with Biro marks on it and thrust it into her hand, too embarrassed to wipe her streaming face himself.

Sobbing quietly, Beverley dabbed at her own face. It felt hot and swollen. Her throat hurt.

'Come and sit on this rock here,' said Kevin quietly. 'Come and look at the seals.'

Beverley's nose felt very warm and tingly, and even her lips were zinging. She felt she'd made a dreadful fool of herself, all that screaming and crying over nothing. She looked up, expecting to see the cliff they'd just climbed down towering above her. But it wasn't. It was just a few feet over her head. Kevin had been right. It was only a piddling little cliff, not dangerous at all, if you were careful. How could she have been so silly about it? She blew her nose, burying her embarrassment in the tissue. Kevin was talking again. But he wasn't saying anything about the idiot she had made of herself. Moments ago, she had hated him for insisting on climbing down, and then she had hated him even more intensely for laughing. But now she was grateful for his tact. He was talking about the seals.

'They're lovely, aren't they Beverley? Sleek. Do you think they are really wet and slimy to touch, or would they be soft and furry? I think maybe soft and furry, myself. I'd say the water just rolls off them.'

Beverley gave her nose a last swipe and then, tucking the paper handkerchief into her pocket, she let Kevin nudge her across the little beach to a smooth rock at the edge of the sea. The seals lay here and there on the beach, within yards of them, and regarded them lazily, only half-curiously.

Beverley hunched on the rock, warm now with the gathered heat of a morning's worth of sun, and gazed at them. She knew vaguely that she was going to have to climb back up that cliff again. But for now, all she wanted to do was stare at these big, lumbering, almost prehistoric-looking creatures, half-animal, half-fish, and listen to the sound of her own heartbeat slowly returning to its normal rhythm.

Chapter 9

KEVIN'S TALE

'DO YOU SEE THAT BIT OF CLIFF BEYOND, the bit that's sticking out?' said Kevin to Beverley, kicking his runners off and rolling his jeans up as far as they would go, which was to a point just below his knees. 'I'm going to wade out around it. I don't think it's deep.'

'No, Kevin, please,' wailed Beverley. She heard herself saying this, pleading with Kevin not to leave her, and she could hardly believe her ears. She didn't even like this person. In fact, she thought she actively disliked him, with his leather jacket and his haircut. But he was all she had. She couldn't bear it if he left her here on her own, with only the seals for company. She looked at them, romping on the beach, rolling over luxuriously in the sun, making satisfied honking noises to each other. She wished she could join them, rolling and flopping and laughing hoarsely.

'I won't be long,' said Kevin. 'I promise I won't.'

Beverley shrugged her shoulders and went on watching the seals, their gleaming coats stretched over rolls of fat. She would pretend Kevin wasn't going. She wouldn't think about it.

She heard him splashing into the water. Still she didn't look, just gritted her teeth and concentrated on the seals. A curious one heaved and humped its way along the shore towards her. She sat very still and hoped it would come right up to her. It came close enough for her to see its surprisingly small face, like a weasel's, its whiskers quivering. She spoke to it in a soft voice, and it sat back on its elbows and cocked its head, like a hard-of-hearing person concentrating on listening. Beverley laughed quietly at its antics.

Minutes later, the splashing noises behind her were repeated. Then came soft footsteps in the sand. At last Beverley looked around. Kevin was wet to the waist, water streaming down his trousers, but he had a satisfied grin on his face.

'Some people say the island is named after them,' he said, tilting his head towards the seals.

'You mean Tranarone is,' Beverley corrected him.

'Oh yes, Tranarone is, but the island too. Seals sometimes get mixed up with people, you know. That's where the legends about mermaids come from – sailors seeing animals with fish-like tails and suckling their young thought they were half-human, half-fish. They say the island was named after these mysterious "ladies". That's one explanation anyway.'

'You weren't gone long,' said Beverley, grateful to Kevin for hurrying back. He wasn't all that bad really. He'd been more than nice about her vertigo attack. She had to admit that.

'No. And I was right. There's another beach on the other side of that promontory thing, a much bigger one than this. And there's a much more gradual incline back up onto dry land. We won't have to climb the cliff again after all, just get around to the next beach and then sure it's only a bit of an oul' ramble up the dunes.'

A wave of relief washed over Beverley. Relief sang in her ears, it did a little jig in her toes, it made the corners of her mouth turn up. But she couldn't bring herself to share her relief with Kevin.

'Oh is that all?' she said, her natural sarcasm returning now that she felt safer. 'Piece of cake, obviously. Just a little matter of wading out to sea up to your waist.'

'Oh come on, Beverley,' said Kevin. 'Anyways, it's either that or climb the cliff.'

Why did she persist in being so nasty to him? She must try not to be. He was doing his best. She could see that.

'OK,' she said, taking off her shoes. 'There's no contest, is there? Let's go.'

They held hands going into the water. Beverley flinched at the cold at first, as the water assaulted her sun-warmed feet, but after a few moments she gave up trying to keep dry and allowed herself to enjoy the sensation of the water filling the fabric of her jeans so that she was weighed down and slowed to an almost trance-like wade.

As Kevin had said, it wasn't difficult to negotiate to the next beach, even if they did arrive on it streaming and sopping and with the bottom halves of their bodies heavy with salt and sea-water.

'I don't think my toes have ever been so clean,' Beverley remarked, looking at them, bleached and sodden, like soaked butter beans.

She sat on a rock and splayed her clean toes to expose as much of her skin as possible to the warming air. Kevin sat on the other side of the rock and leant back against her, also turning himself to the sun to dry. They sat there companionably for a while, looking in opposite directions, their spines just touching, like bookends without any books between them. Beverley felt completely relaxed. She wanted to sit here and dry out and not have to move for a long, long time.

'The local people have lots of stories about the seals,' Kevin said. Beverley could feel his voice rumbling along her vertebrae, like a train in the distance.

'Mmm?' said Beverley lazily, her eyes closed against the glare of the sun.

'And they have stories about mermaids, but I think they're really seal stories too.'

'Are *you* going to start now?' Beverley asked, but without much irritation.

'Start what?'

'Telling stories, like Elizabeth.'

'Oh no. I couldn't tell a story. Not as well as Elizabeth. I don't understand where all them words come from.'

'But do you know the stories the local people tell?'

'I do.'

'Tell me one, then.'

'Ah no, I told you, I can't. I don't know how.'

'But if you know the story, all you have to do is just tell it.'

'Oh, I don't think it's as simple as that at all. I'm sure it's not. I'm not good with words.'

'Elizabeth isn't usually much good with words, but when she started, it all just flowed out of her. I think that's the way stories work. If you just start, the story takes over, and you get a different – a different voice I suppose I mean.'

'A special voice for telling stories in?'

'Mmm, yes, a story-telling voice. Go on, try.'

'Ah no,' said Kevin.

All Beverley wanted to do for now was sit still on this rock and listen to Kevin talking and feeling the words running down her back. She didn't much care what he said.

'Go on,' she said lazily.

'Well,' said Kevin.

'Once upon a time,' said Beverley encouragingly.

'Once upon a time,' repeated Kevin. And suddenly he was away: 'Once upon a time there was a mermaid. A family of mermaids. They all lived under the sea.'

'Naturally,' murmured Beverley.

'It was a huge family. A mother mermaid, a father mermaid and eleven children mermaids.'

'You can't have a father mermaid,' Beverley pointed out, never able to let an inaccuracy go, even when she was feeling sleepy and dreamy. 'A male mermaid is a merman.'

'Ah you see, I can't do it. I knew I couldn't. I'm no good with words.' Kevin clammed up.

'No, no, I'm sorry. That's just me. I'll try not to do it again. Just tell the story.'

'I thought you didn't like stories. You got cross when Elizabeth started to tell her story.'

'Yes. No. I don't know. I'd like you to tell me one,' said Beverley shyly. 'Try again.'

'Well,' began Kevin. 'Where was I?'

'Eleven children.'

'Ah yes. There were eleven children mermaids.'

'All girls?'

'No, no, some of them must have been merlads, I suppose. Anyway, these eleven children mermaids all loved their mother most, most, most ...' Kevin was casting around for a word.

'Dreadfully?' Beverley suggested.

'Amazingly,' Kevin amended. 'They danced – no, swam – attendance on her day and night. They read her stories when she couldn't sleep. They sang songs to her on rocks. They brought her the nicest bits of fish to eat when they came home from fishing expeditions.

'But they didn't bother much with their father. You see, he was away a lot, prospecting for gold.'

'Prospecting for gold?' interposed Beverley. 'I didn't think mermaids – or mermen – did things like that. It sounds like a job to me. Oh sorry, I said I wouldn't interrupt.'

'You're all right. It was a job, yes.'

'You can't have a mermaid with a job. It's too earthly.'

'It's not a mermaid, aren't you after telling me that yourself? It's a merman.'

'That doesn't make any difference.'

'Well, anyway, this merman just liked prospecting for gold. He had ...' and again Kevin stopped and searched his mind for a word.

'Go on, what did he have?'

'An adventurous spirit,' said Kevin shyly.

'And what about the mermaid? Did she have job too?'

'She had eleven children. She had her hands full.' This story wasn't working out the way Kevin had planned. 'No, I can't tell it. I just can't make it come out right.'

'You're doing fine. But could I just point out that you said the eleven children did all the work, the fishing and everything.'

'Oh lord!' Kevin ran his fingers through his salted hair, so hard that it made it stick up like a punk's. 'I told you I'm no good at this.'

'Sorry, sorry, sorry. Not another word. Go on.'

'Anyways, they didn't bother so much with their father because they didn't see all that much of him. They kept all their love and attention for their mother, who was very beautiful and charming.

'Now, after a while, the father mermaid – I mean, merman – began to get jealous of his wife. He would come home laden with gold and jewels, diadems and tiaras and things. Brooches and necklaces too, yes, and anklets and bracelets and torcs and lunulae.'

'Laden? Jewels?'

Kevin turned right around to look at Beverley and glared.

'No, no!' she said defensively. 'I'm not really interrupting. I'm just wondering out loud. I'm just wondering what sort of a gold mine has readymade jewels in it, tiaras and lunulae and all those things you said?'

Kevin settled back in his former position.

'It wasn't gold mines he went prospecting in, it was shipwrecks. He would swim way down into the ribby holds. He would slither past skeletons wearing tatters of clothes and leather belts with cutlasses still in place and stiff old shoes. They'd be all hunched up, these skeletons, under the curve of the boat, with their bony arms clasped around their bony legs.'

'Ooh,' said Beverley with a quick shiver.

'Anyways, our friend the mermaid, the merman, I mean, he'd find their treasure chests. Pirate ships were best. They had lots of loot. But merchant ships had rich pickings too. If there weren't any treasure chests or heavy iron safes, he would sort of *waft* in among the skeletons and slip the gold rings off their skeleton fingers, and he'd lift golden chains up over their skulls, and he'd unbuckle the gold buckles at their bony waists.'

'I thought you said you couldn't tell a story!'

'Shush. You'll spoil the flow. Where was I? Oh yes, he would drape the jewels all over his body. A tiara on his head, necklaces around his neck, rings on his fingers, bracelets and anklets too snaking up his arms. Then he would swim slowly and majestically home, weighed down with the wealth he had stolen.

'He would bring all this gold and these diamonds and emeralds, amethysts and lapis lazula, rubies and quartzite and tigerstones and amber, and he would heap them at the feet – I mean at the tail – of his lovely wife.

'But his wife had no interest in gold or rubies or diamonds. She rumbled around in his offerings, picking up first one trinket and then another, and then she would throw it away as if it were a worthless bauble.

'"Ah," she would sigh, "husband, why do you bring me these things? These are the riches of the earth. What are they to me who has the wide ocean to play in and the wind in my hair and my eleven wonderful children to swim attendance on me day and night and bring me tasty morsels till I am satiated?"'

'Satiated! That's a good word.'

'And then she would turn away from him and start to comb a child's hair. Her children's hair was finer than any gold her husband brought her. It was butter-red and silken-streamy and it gave her more pleasure to comb it with a simple whalebone comb than to look at any of the treasures her merman husband could bring to her.

'The merman would swim off sadly to a distant rock and comb his own butter-red, silken-streamy hair. Nobody ever offered to comb it for him any more.

'One day, while he was prospecting away as usual in a pirate ship, the merman had a thought. He would run away – swim away – from home. Nobody would even miss him, he thought. So he shook his jewels off his body, unwound gold chains from round his neck and chest and slithered out of bangles, letting the jewels drop from him and twirl slowly down to the ocean bed and sink into the murky sands at the bottom of the sea. And then off he swam to seek his fortune.

'That evening, as it grew dark, and the mermaid children gathered around their mother on her favourite rock and had their fish supper, a storm started to brew up on the ocean. It started with a frown on the horizon and just a hint of laciness on the surface of the sea, but the mother mermaid recognised the signs.

'"Eat up quickly, children," she urged. "Let's get finished before this storm reaches us."

'So the children stuffed the remaining fish into their mouths and scooped up handfuls of seawater to wash it down, and then they all twelve dived off the rock and swam down, down, into the depths of the ocean, and right into a special cavern which they used in times of storm as a shelter. It was so deep in the ocean that no storm could reach them there.

'For three days and three nights, the storm raged above them. They could hear it as a distant rumble, the mermaid family, deep down in their storm-proof cavern, and when they swam to the mouth of the cavern and looked out, all they could see was dark night all around them, so they knew the storm clouds still filled the sky and prevented the sun from getting through. Only occasionally, the gloom was relieved by streaks of sudden light, followed by muffled booming sounds. That was part of the storm, their mother said.

'The mermaids' storm cavern was so deep down in the ocean that no fishes ever swam near. And so the mermaids had nothing to eat for the three long days and nights while they huddled there. At first they didn't mind, as they'd had such a good supper the night the storm had whipped up. But by morning they were starting to get hungry. And when there was still no sign of the storm abating by lunchtime the next day, they began to get very unsettled in themselves.

'By the evening of the first day, the smallest mermaid children were starting to whimper with hunger pangs, and by the evening of the second day, one of them whined: "Where's Papa? I want my papa!" And by the evening of the third day, all the children were wailing for their lost papa. They seemed to think that if their father would only come the storm would be over and they would get some food.

'But their father didn't come.

'On the morning of the fourth day, there was a glimmer at the mouth of the cavern, just a greeniness in the water, not anything you would recognise as light, but the mother mermaid knew it meant that the clouds had started to break up, way up miles above in the sky, and so she called out to the children that they could leave the cave. They all swam together to the mouth of the storm cave, and they started to swim slowly, with weak movements of their arms and tails, up to the surface of the water.

'Before very long, the family of mermaids had got over their miserable stay in the cave. They had fished and fished and eaten and eaten until they were well and strong again, but still their father hadn't come home. The children still missed him, and they still wailed for him in the evenings, especially in that last hour before supper when they were hungry.

'Years went by, and the mother mermaid was weary by now of always being a mother and always having eleven children and never having a husband to help her. Even she missed her husband now, and when the children started up their evening wailing, she too would sometimes wipe a tear away.

'Then one evening, the merman came home. He swam up to the rock at supper time, just as his wife was combing her youngest child's hair.

'"Dear wife," he said, "how I have missed you and our eleven lovely children. I just had to come home this once and see you all again."

'His wife stared at him, glad to see him but wondering what he meant by "this once".

'The children all came swimming around their father and covered him with salty kisses and begged to know where he had been.

'Well, he told them that he was after making a new life for himself, that he had a new family now, on the dry land. He said his new wife loved it when he left his earthly home and came back laden with jewels mined from the ocean deep.

'But he said he was sometimes filled with longing to see his old family again, and his old wife, and so he had come on a short visit.

'They all wept to hear it was only to be a short visit, but he explained to them that because he had married an earth-woman he had lost his merman's tail and grown human legs. He said he only had his tail now between dusk and dawn, and during the day he had to live on the land and breathe the air, like humans.

'Sadly, they all had to accept that he could no longer live the life of a merman and be with them, but they made him promise to come and see them just sometimes, when he wasn't too busy prospecting for gold for his earthly family.

'As the merman was about to leave, he produced a present for his mermaid wife. It was a single jewel. But it was a jewel such as she had never seen before. It was milky white with blue and pink lights glimmering on its surface.

'"Ah!" she exclaimed, holding it up on the palm of her hand. "At last you bring me a treasure of the earth that I find beautiful."

'"Oh no, wife," he replied. "That is no treasure of the earth.

That is a treasure of the sea."

'And with that he kissed his wife lovingly and he kissed each of his eleven children and said goodbye to them all.

'Then he swam slowly away from them, and they were left with nothing but longing in their hearts and a single memento of their father – a beautiful, glowing pearl.'

Chapter 10

THE LUNCH THAT
DISAPPEARED – TWICE

BEVERLEY DIDN'T KNOW WHAT TO SAY. She had obviously completely underestimated this boy, but she didn't know how to tell him what a terrific storyteller she thought he was. At last she managed to say 'That was a lovely story,' in a small, embarrassed voice. 'Thank you,' she added, hoping she was saying the right thing.

'Yeah, well, I don't know where it came from really,' said Kevin, looking embarrassed too.

'All that stuff about treasures of the earth and treasures of the sea and the silken-streamy hair and everything! You must be a bit of a poet.'

'Yeh! Without knowing it!' said Kevin with an awkward laugh. Then he changed the subject: 'Lookit, I bet if we climb up these dunes, we should be able to walk around the island and maybe meet up with the other pair. And sure even if we don't, we'll arrive back on that beach we landed on this morning, in time for dinner. I mean, lunch.'

'Mmmm,' said Beverley, patting her trousers to see if they were dry. They weren't dry. In fact, they were still sopping wet. 'Sounds good. I'm ravenous.'

Their progress was slow, hampered by the wetness of their clothing and the difficulty of walking barefoot and on sand, but they made it up the dunes and then walked, their lower halves still gently steaming, along the dry and spiky marram grass, until they met a familiar-looking path, with a streak of daisies down the middle of it.

'This must be Gerard and Elizabeth's trail,' said Beverley, straining to see if she could make out their figures in the distance. But the view along the path was limited to a few yards. After that, the path disappeared into a green tunnel of hedgerow and undergrowth and overhanging bushes.

Kevin threw a worried look along the trail. How far had they got? he wondered. And had they met the island woman – the Witch of Lady Island as some of the Tranarone people called her? But he didn't mention his fears to Beverley. It might be all OK. They might not have met her, and even if they had, well ...

After dripping along the trail for some time, they spotted a bright and alien object flung carelessly across the path, something long and spindly and wrapped in disintegrating coloured paper – a garden flare.

'Aha!' said Beverley, pouncing on it. 'They've been here. Where's ours, by the way?'

'I suppose it must be back on the cliff,' said Kevin, 'with the lunch rucksack.'

'Oh no!' wailed Beverley. 'And my sum copy!' She could hardly believe she hadn't missed it earlier. She hadn't felt the urge to record a single thing, not since the lark.

Her wet jeans felt cold now, her feet weren't clean any more – bits of leaf and grit and grass and sand clung to them and irritated her between her toes – but they were too damp still to coax back into her runners, and her hair felt full of creatures, though she knew it was just perspiration running along her scalp that caused that sensation. And now an overwhelming pang of hunger punched her right in the middle and almost knocked the breath out of her.

'Ah well,' said Kevin, 'Gerard and Elizabeth have to be near here somewhere. Sure we'll find them soon, and then we can all get back to the beach for a bite to eat. And after that we can head off home.' With a bit of luck, they'd get off the island safe and sound and none the worse for their adventures.

'No, we can't do that,' Beverley pointed out. 'We can't leave until the next low tide. Unless you expect us to swim!'

'Oh lord!' said Kevin, running his hands through his hair. He hadn't thought about that. How could he possibly have forgotten? And now what was he going to do? How could he keep them out of the woman's way all day?

Within yards, and around a bend that had hidden her from view only a moment ago, they almost stumbled across the recumbent form of Elizabeth, who appeared to have dozed off, right in the middle of the pathway. What a silly place to choose for a nap, thought Beverley, disapprovingly, though she knew of course that it didn't really matter, as there weren't any cars on the island to come and run her over.

'Where's Gerard?' Beverley asked, sinking to the ground beside Elizabeth.

Groggily, Elizabeth levered herself onto one elbow and parted her hair – long since loosened from its plait – and peered out of it at Beverley. Then she winced, remembering her ankle as she woke up.

'Gone back to the beach,' she muttered. 'He went to meet you two. And to get some supplies. It must be nearly lunchtime. I'm starving.' She was fully awake now, and her voice was getting clearer. 'In fact, I was starving a good half-an-hour ago. We didn't have any elevenses.'

Elevenses! Only Elizabeth could expect elevenses on a deserted island in the middle of the Atlantic ocean, inhabited by half-human seals and full of terrifying cliffs. In spite of herself, Beverley smiled. Still, she didn't think it was a good idea for Elizabeth to have fallen asleep in the middle of what amounted to the road and let Gerard go roaming off over the island on his own. He was only eleven after all. And his health wasn't great.

'Why didn't you go with him?' she asked bossily.

'Because of this!' announced Elizabeth dramatically, pointing at her ankle, which by now had puffed up like a weird and horrible mushroom. 'I tried crawling for a bit, but I got tired and my clothes started to tear. I must have fallen asleep. Was I asleep?'

'Yes,' said Beverley, examining the damaged ankle. 'You've given this a right twist, haven't you?'

'It hurts like anything,' said Elizabeth, 'but only if I try to move it. Oh Beverley,' she went on, her voice rising anxiously, 'you don't think we could get sort of stuck inside a story, do you?'

'What do you mean?'

'My story, the one I told this morning, about the four children and one of them hurting her leg. It's sort of coming true, isn't it?'

'Rubbish, Elizabeth. You're letting your imagination run away with you.'

'Don't you think there's a parallel?' Elizabeth found it usually worked if you used scientific-sounding language with Beverley. It made her take you more seriously.

It worked.

'Well, I suppose there *is* a parallel,' Beverley agreed, 'but it doesn't mean anything. It's just a coincidence.' Beverley was a great believer in coincidence. She found it explained a lot of mysteries. Beverley didn't like mysteries.

'All the same,' said Elizabeth dramatically, 'I don't think anyone should tell any stories about people being stranded on desert islands and starving to death and their bones being bleached in the sun.'

'Don't be silly, Liz. This isn't a desert island, and there is absolutely no danger of anything bleaching in the sun in this climate.'

'It's warm today,' Elizabeth pointed out lugubriously.

'Just a fluke.'

Kevin broke into the girls' conversation: 'Here comes Gerard.' He was standing up and had a better view down the green-dark tunnel of the path. He could just spot Gerard, a multi-coloured blur jogging along in the distance.

'We could do with some of those wishberries now,' said Elizabeth. 'Mine would be tomato-sandwich-flavoured.'

'No, we couldn't,' said Beverley briskly. She felt in control again, now that there was a little crisis to rise to. 'Gerard's on his way. He'll have the food rucksack. We'll have a lovely picnic and then we'll have a think about what we're going to do about your ankle.'

Gerard came closer. They could hear the pounding of his feet on the grassy path. Pretty soon they could hear his breathing, heavy and gasping. His hair was plastered to his forehead with sweat and his glasses were all steamed up. He gave off unpleasant odours as he flung himself down beside Elizabeth and drew in huge, gulping breaths. There was no sign of the food rucksack.

Gerard carried nothing on his back but his hooded sweatshirt, the sleeves knotted loosely around his neck.

'What happened you, Gerard?' asked Kevin in alarm. 'Didn't you make it as far as the beach? Are you all right? Is somebody after chasing you?'

He fired out these questions at Gerard, but he wasn't looking at him. He was peering in the direction Gerard had come from, half expecting to see a mad witch flying along after him waving a wand, or at least a stick.

Gerard nodded vigorously. Then he shook his head for good measure. He drew in an extra large gulp of air and spat it out again. With the outbreath came a spate of words:

'Yes. Yes. No. Nobody. Just – had – to – run – Elizabeth – didn't want – to – leave her – long. The tide – ' Here he stopped again and took a few more long gulps of air. Elizabeth slapped him encouragingly on the back.

'The tide,' went on Gerard after a bit, 'it's come in. Right up the beach. It's buried everything. All the food and stuff. Everything has just disappeared.'

'Oh no!' Everyone suddenly felt hungrier than ever at this news.

'Not so much as a biscuit left,' said Gerard dramatically. His breathing had settled down now, and he hadn't had to use his inhaler.

'But if the tide took it,' reasoned Beverley, 'then surely at least some of it must be floating on the water. Let's go and fish it out and see what we can save. At least the tinned stuff couldn't be too badly damaged.'

'No,' said Gerard. 'I'm telling you, there's no point. There isn't a single thing left. *Nothing* is floating on the water.'

'Well, then, the tide *can't* have taken it,' argued Beverley. She looked around at the others for their opinion.

Elizabeth and Kevin exchanged a look. They'd both had the same thought. Maybe the tide hadn't taken the food after all. Maybe it had been a person who'd taken it. A person who didn't appreciate her island being invaded by outsiders.

'Everything is gone,' Gerard went on, as if to make quite sure they'd all understood him. 'Rucksacks, food, spare clothes, saucepans, everything.'

'I *said* it would be good to have some wishberries,' wailed Elizabeth. 'And I was right! O-o-o-h! Just think of all our lovely food drifting off on the waves!' She glared at Kevin as she said this, as if warning him not to mention the possibility that had crossed both their minds.

'Ah sure maybe the seals will find it,' said Kevin, playing along.

'What seals?' asked Elizabeth, but nobody bothered to answer her.

'Most of it wouldn't be much good to them,' said Beverley, who always saw the logical flaws in things, 'unless they have developed the knack of using their flippers as tin-openers.'

'I wish we had those boiled eggs,' moaned Elizabeth.

'And the bananas,' added Gerard sadly. He was very fond of bananas.

'It's not even autumn,' said Beverley, pulling lumps of tattered curls through her fingers in a characteristic gesture of distress.

'How do you mean?' asked Elizabeth.

'You know, blackberries, mushrooms, that sort of thing.'

'Haws,' added Kevin absently.

'*Haws*!' yelped Elizabeth. 'You can't eat haws, can you?'

'Indeed and you can,' said Kevin, who went in for nature, 'if you're hungry. They don't taste great, though,' he added honestly.

'I don't think I could ever be hungry enough to eat haws,' said Elizabeth, wrinkling her nose.

'I could be,' said Gerard. 'In fact, I think I probably am. If there were any. But wait – what about that lunch Elizabeth packed? Beverley and Kevin, you took that rucksack, didn't you? What happened to it? Don't tell me you've eaten it all?'

'No, no,' said Kevin. 'We didn't eat it – it sort of got lost. I mean, eh, we know where it is, but it's beyond on the other side of the island.' He didn't mention the vertigo attack, Beverley noticed, and she was grateful he didn't blame her.

Nobody volunteered to go and get the rucksack. They were all too hot, despondent, hungry.

'We could fish,' said Gerard vaguely.

'With this garden candle, flare, whatever you call it, I suppose,' said Elizabeth tartly.

'Umm,' conceded Gerard. It hadn't been a very bright idea really.

'Or harvest snails,' said Elizabeth excitedly, 'like French people.'

'No, we couldn't do that,' Beverley pointed out. 'You have to feed them flour to clean out their insides, and we haven't got any of that.'

'Sand might do,' suggested Gerard.

'Well, it *might* work,' said Beverley, practically, 'but I don't see how you could get them to eat it.'

'I don't think I like this island very much,' said Elizabeth, pouting. Her ankle was throbbing, and she was hungry, and she had this weird feeling that somebody was watching them all the time, and now there was no food and no way of getting any, not even snails or haws, and she didn't see how she was going to walk home. She wished she had never agreed to Beverley's putrid plan. She knew all along there was something spooky about this place, and she was just about to say so, when Gerard spoke.

'There's always the emergency chocolate rations,' he said tentatively, half-afraid the girls would jump on him for suggesting such a thing in what wasn't exactly a life-and-death situation.

'Gerard, you genius!' exclaimed Beverley unexpectedly. 'You absolute angel! You're absolutely stupendous, that's what you are!'

'Am I?' asked Gerard, pleased, taking out his chocolate bar. It was a write-off – all melted and distorted from his hot and sweaty run. Kevin's was only partially melted, and Beverley's was quite respectable. Elizabeth's was in the best condition. She had taken off her jacket and flung it in the cool ditch, so the chocolate had hardly melted at all.

'Let's eat mine,' Elizabeth suggested, 'and put Kevin's and Beverley's in the ditch to cool off. I suppose we could put this mangled mess of Gerard's in the ditch too, and if we get really desperate we could sort of suck it out of the silver paper.'

'Good idea,' agreed Beverley, already dividing Elizabeth's chocolate ration into four.

Everyone took their share gratefully. They ate it carefully, savouring the sweet ooze of it in their mouths.

'This is nice,' said Gerard, 'isn't it?'

'Oh yes, it's great,' said Elizabeth sarcastically. 'Here we are stuck on an island. I can't walk. I can't even get very far on all fours. We have no food except some chocolate. It's very nice chocolate, but it's not exactly lunch, is it? And we haven't got anything to drink either. This is just nice and cosy, Gerard, sure it is. It's just great. I vote we do this every day.'

'Oh shut up, Elizabeth,' snapped Beverley. 'Things are bad enough without you pointing it out like that.'

'I'm only telling the truth,' said Elizabeth huffily.

'Let ye not be arguing,' said Kevin. 'Come on now, lads, we're going to have to stay friends. We're going to have to think up a plan.'

'Yes,' said Beverley, not wanting the leadership of the little group to slip away to Kevin. 'Yes, Kevin's right. We need a bit of co-operation around here, not fighting.'

Elizabeth threw her eyes up to heaven. Look who's talking, she thought.

'We need water,' said Gerard. 'But I'm tired. I'm too tired to go and look for any.'

'I'm tired too, Gerard,' said Beverley. 'Look, why don't we all have a bit of a rest, and then we can go and look for water.'

Nobody objected to the idea of a rest. It sounded even more attractive just now than a drink of water. At the very idea of a rest, they all gathered more closely together and huddled in a little group in the shade of the hawthorn hedge out of the heat of the noonday sun. Beverley threw a jacket over Elizabeth, because she thought she might be in shock.

'What about another story?' Kevin ventured, looking tentatively at Beverley. 'Just to relax us all.'

'That's a great idea,' said Elizabeth. 'Gerard can tell.'

Gerard reddened with pleasure.

'*I* think this is just like *The Canterbury Tales*,' Elizabeth went on. 'We're like pilgrims, aren't we?'

'Wha-at?' asked Kevin, who'd never heard of Canterbury or its tales.

'You know, the pilgrims in *The Canterbury Tales* – they all tell each other stories. This is just like that, a pilgrimage with stories.'

'It's not a pilgrimage,' said Beverley firmly. 'It's an expedition.'

'Well, *I'm* playing that it's a pilgrimage,' countered Elizabeth complacently.

'Huh!' said Beverley, who at thirteen was working hard to eliminate the word 'play' from her vocabulary. Elizabeth was a whole year younger, so that explained why she had such an immature outlook.

'And now we even have a sick,' added Elizabeth in a satisfied tone.

'What?' asked all the others, slightly disgusted.

'A sick,' explained Elizabeth. 'You're supposed to take the sick on pilgrimages. I'm the sick.'

'Oh yuck!' said Gerard.

'Yes,' said Elizabeth, warming to her idea. 'And maybe we'll have a miracle. Maybe I'll be miraculously healed and you'll all be witnesses and somebody will be canonised.'

'Who?' asked Beverley skeptically.

'I don't know,' Elizabeth admitted. 'But anyway, go on, tell the story, Gerard. We're all ears.'

Gerard hesitated. He looked at Beverley pleadingly.

'Go on, so, Gerard,' said Beverley. She'd got over her inhibitions about stories. In fact, she thought, this was a good way to postpone worrying about their situation just a bit longer.

And so they all settled down together in the shade of the hedgerow, like little birds nestling on their night perches, to listen to a story.

Chapter 11

GERARD'S TALE

GERARD DREW IN A BREATH, swallowed some chocolate and began: 'Once there was a young woman. Well, a girl, really; she was like a princess, or an heiress, or something. Very rich, very good family. When she was fourteen, her father made her get engaged – what do they call it in stories?'

'Betrothed?' Elizabeth suggested.

'Yes, that's it, thank you, betrothed. He betrothed her to a young man from another good family, a family he wanted to make an alliance with. The girl hadn't met the young man. It was an arranged marriage. But she didn't mind. That was how she had been brought up. She didn't know any different.'

'Huh!' said Elizabeth.

'Hmph!' said Beverley.

'Because she was only fourteen, it was agreed that it would be a fairly long engagement. Her fiancé wouldn't come to claim her until her sixteenth birthday. In the meantime, she could finish out her girlhood, learn the things she needed to know in order to be a wife, and adjust to the idea of marriage.'

'Grrr!' said Elizabeth.

'Crumbs!' said Beverley. Was this boy only eleven? Where did he get these ideas from?

'The girl was quite excited about it all. Getting married was a very important step in a girl's life.'

'Oh my!' said Beverley, shaking her head.

'Rats!' said Elizabeth, through gritted teeth.

'Give over, you two,' said Gerard. 'You're spoiling it.'

'Well, it's a stupid story,' said Elizabeth.

'No, it's not. It's just the way things were in those days.'

'Oh well, in *those* days,' said Elizabeth, giving in, because she wanted to hear what happened next.

'Getting married,' Gerard went on carefully, challenging Elizabeth with a frown not to interrupt him again, 'was when she stopped being a child and started to live the life of an adult. She looked forward to that. She would have her own house, and her own servants, and she would be in charge. And some day, she would have babies of her own too, and that would also be nice, better than dolls. This was how she was thinking. But she hardly thought at all about the young man she was supposed to be marrying. You see, she had never met a young man before, and had no idea what to expect. The only man she had ever known was her father, and he only came to see her on her birthdays, and anyway he was old, with a beard and a pot belly. So the girl concentrated on thinking about the house and servants and children she would have, and didn't think at all about the husband.

'One day, just before her fifteenth birthday, she was out riding in the woods, which she liked to do most days. She loved riding along as fast as her horse would go, leaping over fallen tree trunks, feeling her long black hair streaming in the wind behind her and being gently brushed back from her face by the twiggy hands of the forest.'

'Mmm,' said Elizabeth. This sounded better.

'Yes,' agreed Beverley.

Only Kevin heard a soft, soft echoing 'Mmm', or thought he did. He looked around carefully, but there was nobody to be seen.

'This particular day, as she was skimming along over the forest floor, she met another rider coming towards her. This rider was as swift as she was, and before long they met on the narrow woodland path. The girl reined in her horse as they came close, and the other rider did the same. Soon they were face to face.

'Well, the girl had never seen such a face as the face of the other rider. It was a handsome, golden-skinned face, and when it smiled, it was like the sun breaking through a cloud. She sat on horseback and stared at the rider. When he put out his hand to her, she dismounted without thinking and allowed the other rider to swing her up onto his horse, and away the pair of them galloped through the woods.

'As soon as she dismounted and rode off with the stranger, the girl's horse turned around and trotted off back home.

'When the horse arrived back at the girl's house without the girl, her father called together all his henchmen, and they went searching the woods for the lost daughter. For three days and three nights they searched, and at last they found her, in the golden-skinned horseman's arms, under a tree.

'The girl's father immediately dismounted, wrenched his daughter from the arms of her lover, threw her across the saddle of his horse and slapped the horse's haunches to make it go, with a cry of "Go home. Go home. Take her and go home." The horse obediently trotted off with the girl hanging, weeping, over its saddle, and the father drew his sword and challenged the golden-skinned stranger to a fight.

'The stranger hopped up and drew his own sword, and with a

few swift strokes he had chopped off the raging father's arms, legs and head and left the bleeding pieces on the forest floor. Then he put up his sword and walked away to his own home.

'When the horse carrying the daughter arrived back at home, the girl's mother came running out and gently lifted her daughter down and brought her indoors.

'The father of course never came home, which was no loss to the girl or her mother. Nobody in the family had ever liked him much, and nobody went looking for him either. The bleeding pieces of his body are probably lying about in the woods still, for all I know.

'Anyway, after some months it turned out that the young girl was going to have a baby. Now, this was a terrible disgrace, as young girls without husbands were not supposed to have babies in that country and at that time. The girl herself was happy enough about the baby, but her mother wanted to keep this terrible disgrace hidden, so she kept the daughter in the house all the time she was pregnant and would not let her meet her friends or talk to anyone.

'When the baby was born, the girl's mother took the little scrap away and told her daughter the child had been born dead. The girl was dreadfully upset at first, but after a while she began to get better and to look forward to the wedding. She would be sixteen very soon now, and her fiancé would come for her.

'Meanwhile, the grandmother took the baby and looked for a place to hide it, so people wouldn't know about the shameful thing that had happened in the family. She crept out of the palace one night and put the baby in the cowshed with the cows, where it would be warm and would have milk to drink, and she left it there and never went back.

'Imagine the surprise and delight of the girl on her wedding day when her bridegroom turned out to be the handsome stranger she had met in the woods, and who was the father of her child!

'On their wedding night, the girl told her husband the whole story, and he was furious to think that his child had been allowed to die. The next morning, he went to his mother-in-law and asked her where the baby was buried, so that he could erect a cross of mother-of-pearl to the child.

'The mother-in-law at first told lie after lie about where the baby was buried, but every lie was so unbelievable that at last the son-in-law winkled the truth out of her, that the child had been sent to live in the byre with the cows.

'In a dreadful rage he left the palace and crossed the yard to where the farm animals were kept, and he searched every shed and outhouse till he found where the cows lived, and there he found a tiny baby, just a few months old, lying curled up in a bed of straw, with a mother cow bending over her and licking her with long, milky, moo-cow licks. He snatched the child up from the floor of the cowshed and brought her back into the castle.

'But as soon as her father lifted her up, the baby started to roar, and she roared and cried all the way back across the yard and all the way through the corridors of the palace to her mother's bedroom, where her mother was undressing for bed.

'"What's this?" cried the bride, jumping up from her dressing table and looking aghast at the brown, smelly, roaring heap of rags and straw he brought with him.

'"This is our daughter!" said her husband, proudly presenting his wife with the bundle.

'"No, it's not," screamed his wife, backing away in disgust. "It's a calf. It's a little sucky calf! Can't you hear it mooing?"

'And sure enough, the baby's cries were not like baby cries at all, but long, mournful moos. The baby was crying for its cow-mother.

'The bridegroom got the servants to bring a silver basket and silk robes for his daughter to sleep in, but all night she mooed and bellowed, and all the next day, and all the next day and night too. The baby kept up its roaring and bellowing for a solid week, and all this time it refused every sort of food. At the end of the week, the father had to let the child go back to its home in the cowshed in case it died of hunger. And so the child grew up among the cattle and never learnt to speak or to read or even to walk on her legs like a human being.

'But every evening, her human father would leave the palace and cross the yard to the cowshed and dandle his daughter on his knee, and there in the warm safety of the byre the child would laugh up into her father's face, and the father knew that his child was happy with this strange animal life, and he never again tried to make her live the life of a normal human child.

'But his wife, knowing now that her child was alive and well, but living among the beasts of the stall, never had a day's happiness, and she died soon afterwards of a broken heart.'

Chapter 12

A STRANGE CARAVAN
LUMBERS FORWARD

'WEE-IIRD!' WHISPERED KEVIN.

'Aaah!' sighed someone. Nobody knew who. The children looked at each other for a moment, and each one wondered which of the others it was. But no one asked. Perhaps they were afraid. Perhaps they thought that if they asked, it would turn out not to be any of them. But if it wasn't any of them, then who was it? Perhaps it was just a little sea breeze, soughing in the hawthorn hedge.

There was silence for a while. Then Elizabeth spoke.

'I don't like the ending,' she said, and she spoke for all three of Gerard's listeners. 'Does she have to die?'

'Yes,' said Gerard. 'That's part of it.'

'Could you not change it?'

'No,' replied Gerard. 'That's the way it happened.'

'What do you mean, that's the way it happened?' asked Beverley. 'It's only a story after all.'

'It's not *only* a story,' said Gerard, with much more authority than he had in real life. 'It's a story, and that's how it ends. She dies.'

'But you made the story up, so you can change the ending if

you want to,' argued Beverley, who shared Elizabeth's opinion about the ending.

'No,' said Gerard strenuously, 'it doesn't *work* like that. I made it up, but *that's* the way I made it up, with that ending, so that's the way it is. If you want to change the ending for yourself, well, I suppose you can, but then it's a different story.'

Elizabeth shrugged. She'd never known Gerard to be so vehement before.

'Oh well, so what?' said Kevin, sensing strain here and trying to sound cheerful. 'As Beverley says, it's only a story.'

He was more concerned with their real plight than with whether or not a story had a happy ending. It didn't seem to have occurred to the others, but Kevin was aware that they were pretty well trapped on this island. First of all, they were trapped by the tide. They hadn't a hope of getting back to the mainland until evening. Secondly, they were trapped by Elizabeth's lameness. How could they possibly get her back across the causeway in the brief space of time the tide would be fully out, if she couldn't walk? Thirdly, not only were they trapped and without food, but he knew that there was at least one other person on this island too – a very peculiar person, maybe not dangerous, but certainly not predictable. And he couldn't help feeling that not only was she on the island, but that she knew they were here too.

'Uh-huh,' Elizabeth was saying, disagreeing with Beverley about the story. 'It's too late now, but I think we should have a rule about nobody dying in any of our stories. Just in case.'

'Just in case what?' asked Kevin, his voice gone to a squeak with apprehension.

But Elizabeth didn't want to explain her theory that you might get stuck inside a story, and if people died in the story, then you might never come out of it again. She didn't want to spook them all. She shivered, though, and bent over her sore foot to hide the expression in her eyes.

The sunny warmth they had enjoyed all morning and which had dried Beverley's and Kevin's jeans to a strange and salty stiffness had stultified now to a dead and heavy heat. Beverley looked at the sky. It had clouded over considerably in the last half-hour. Where before there had been blue with sprigs of clouds tripping across it, as if for decoration rather than with any serious intention of rain, now the clouds had started to mass and push their way, greying gradually and with steady determination, across the expanse of blue, and threatened to engulf it completely before long.

'Rain on the way,' said Beverley scientifically. There was something comforting in her matter-of-factness about natural phenomena. Beverley wasn't one for believing you could get stuck in a story or be watched by a secretive witch.

Kevin looked up at the sky and saw a storm written across its face. He shivered and drew his jacket around him, though it was very warm.

'Cumulus clouds,' Beverley went on, 'always a bad sign. That's all we need! Look, we really must do something about Elizabeth's foot. It looks gross. We need to try and get the swelling down if we can.'

'My mother uses ice,' said Elizabeth, regarding her deformed ankle with tenderness mixed with foreboding.

'The next best thing to ice would be running water,' said Beverley. 'A stream would be ideal. Or the sea. Maybe we could get you to the beach to bathe it.'

'Wait a minute!' cried Gerard. 'I saw a house on my way to the beach. Where there's a house there must be a water supply. And it would be much closer than going all the way back to the beach. Anyway, you can't drink seawater, and I need a drink.'

'A house!' exclaimed Elizabeth. 'You couldn't have seen a house, Gerard. You went back along the same path we came on this morning. We didn't pass any house then.'

Gerard thought for a moment. 'I'm sure I saw one,' he said slowly, wondering.

A house! That had to be *her* house, Kevin was sure of it. Well, they couldn't go to *that* house, anyway. Although at least a house was some sort of sign of normality. He had been half-afraid she might live in a cave or a tree-house or something outlandish.

'Why don't we try to make for there?' Gerard was saying eagerly, glad to have discovered something useful, 'and see if they have a tap or something?'

'It's made of gingerbread, I suppose!' Elizabeth tried to inject scorn into her voice, but she was half-afraid that Gerard was going to reply that now she mentioned it, yes, it was actually made of gingerbread. She didn't like the idea of meeting this strange person that Kevin had hinted at, though she didn't like to admit it.

Kevin made a small strangled sound in his throat. Beverley absentmindedly clapped him on the back, as if to clear a blockage in his oesophagus, but she wasn't really paying much attention to Kevin. She was far more interested in this house of Gerard's.

'It's at a funny angle,' Gerard explained, as he thought harder about the house. 'Yes, that's it. And it's well hidden by trees. It wouldn't be visible from the other direction. All you'd see would be the trees. That's why I saw it on the way back to the beach, but not on my way back here again. Yes, that explains it.'

'So you're quite sure it's not a *magic* house, then, are you

Gerard, one that appears and disappears?' Elizabeth said, half-sarcastic, half-hoping it really was a magic house and had actually disappeared.

'No, of course it isn't. It's a real house, a sort of a biggish cottage, with a slate roof and a chimney.'

'Derelict?' asked Beverley. 'Or not?'

'Mmmmmm.' Gerard was undecided.

Kevin was looking away across the rocks and ditches among which they sat, as if he didn't belong to this party of lost children at all.

'A bit overgrown and neglected-looking all right,' said Gerard. 'I mean there wasn't a car outside and somebody dead-heading the roses or anything. No sign of life.'

'Curtains?' asked Beverley.

Kevin continued to look away to the horizon.

'N-o-o,' said Gerard. 'But it wasn't exactly falling to bits either. I mean, it looks habitable enough.'

'Right,' said Beverley, standing up and slapping her hands together in her decisive way. 'I vote we head for the house. As Gerard says, a house probably means water, and we could all do with a drink. And anyway, we need to get in out of this rain that's coming. It's going to be heavy.'

'Actually,' said Kevin tentatively, feeling uncomfortable with that word. It sounded like a city-word, a Beverley-word, but he couldn't think of any other way to break into the conversation. 'Actually, I don't think we should go to the house.'

'What! Why ever not?' Beverley sat down again with a plonk on the grass and peered at Kevin.

Kevin looked away at the horizon again, with his shoulders hunched, and said nothing for a long time.

'Well?' went on Beverley, who didn't have much time for moody looks and mysterious shrugs. 'What have you got against this house, Master Kevin?'

'Well ...' said Kevin, looking around. He caught Elizabeth's eye and gave her an appealing look. Help me out, his eyes seemed to say, I can't explain the problem without seeming to be an awful idiot.

'I think,' said Elizabeth, picking up on Kevin's plea, 'I think maybe someone lives there.'

'Oh well, big deal!' said Beverley. 'That's not a reason for keeping away from the house. In fact, it's all the better if someone lives there. They might give us some lunch. They might have a first aid kit or something. They might be able to telephone to the mainland for us.'

First aid kit! Telephone! Really, Beverley hadn't a clue. Kevin tried again: 'I think maybe we wouldn't be welcome.'

'Or maybe we'd be *too* welcome,' added Elizabeth dramatically, mysteriously.

'Too welcome? Oh Elizabeth, grow up! I refuse to believe that someone would want to kidnap us. We're not on television, you know. Or in Sicily.'

Kidnapping sounded not so bad really to Kevin. Kidnapping was nice and predictable. They tied you up and they sent letters to your parents, and somebody paid a ransom and then you got to go home. Just so long as their families could be relied on to pay up and they got to keep their ears and their fingers, kidnapping wouldn't be so bad at all. At least they'd probably get fed. No, what Kevin feared was something spookier than common or garden kidnapping. But exactly what it was he feared he couldn't exactly say.

'What I mean is, the person who lives there, well, she's not the full shilling – a bit odd, you might say.'

'You *know* who lives there?' shrilled Beverley. 'Why didn't you say so? And what do you mean *odd*? Do her socks not match? Does she talk to herself? *Odd* doesn't sound anything to be afraid of.'

'I didn't say we should be afraid. I just said I didn't think we should go there.'

'Look, Kevin, and you too, Elizabeth,' said Beverley going all reasonable, 'we have a problem here. We have a casualty on our hands. Elizabeth is in a bad way. She can't walk. Her ankle's a mess. We need help. We need a doctor, really, but if we can't have a doctor, a telephone would be a help, or even a stretcher. At the very least we need ice or cold water and a bandage. Also, we're all hungry. A sandwich would be nice too. Or even a cup of tea would make us feel better. And it's going to rain. So I vote, if there's a house, we make for it. We can throw ourselves on the mercy of this odd person. It can't be worse than being caught out here in a rainstorm with a patient who can't move and no lunch and no way of getting home.'

Kevin looked uneasily at Elizabeth, but Elizabeth was looking as confused as he was. Kevin couldn't think of an argument to put up against Beverley's sweet reason, and anyway he didn't want to be out in this storm he was certain was brewing up, so he shrugged and gave in: 'I suppose so,' he said heavily. 'Yeh, I suppose you're right.'

'Is everyone agreed, then, to head for the house?' asked Beverley, in a sudden fit of democracy.

There was a long moment of silence.

'Yes,' said Gerard finally. 'But how are we going to get Elizabeth there? I don't think we could find anything that would do for crutches.'

'Oh, I'll crawl,' said Elizabeth humbly.

'Don't be ridiculous, Liz!' said Beverley. 'Kevin and I will carry you. Gerard will have Fat to worry about.'

'Carry me?' shrieked Elizabeth.

'Fat!' shrieked Gerard, looking about wildly, his breath coming suddenly in short gasps.

'Yes,' said Beverley, in reply to Elizabeth's shriek. 'But not like a stretcher. Like a sedan chair. Look, we both cross our arms, and then we grab each other's hands, to form a seat. Then we hunker down, and Elizabeth sits on the seat, and we lift her up. She can put one arm around my neck and one around yours, Kevin. Didn't you play that game at primary school?'

'Where's Fat?' asked Gerard in a small, sobbing voice, afraid of what the answer was going to be.

'That blasted cat!' said Elizabeth crossly. 'It's all his fault that I fell, you know. I hope that sheep ate him for its lunch.'

Gerard looked at his cousin, but he couldn't see her properly. For some reason, she seemed to be shimmering, as if she were under water. How could she be so cruel? He dared not say anything. He didn't think his voice would be there anyway, if he tried to open his mouth. He blinked hard and Elizabeth swam into focus.

'Shush, Elizabeth,' said Beverley, noticing Gerard's face. It had lost the bright red colour it had had when he'd arrived running back from the beach. In fact, it had lost all colour. It was chalky white and his light brown eyes looked huge in its expanse of white, big and buttery brown and very wet. Soon he was gasping for breath, flailing about with his arms and hunching over.

'Where did you last see him, Ger?' asked Beverley.

Elizabeth was exasperated. It had been all Fat's fault, and now here was Beverley full of concern about that nuisance of an animal. What had come over her? Elizabeth shook her head and blew hard through her nose, but she didn't argue. She didn't think she was in a position to.

'In the field, over that hedge,' said Gerard, pointing desperately, his inhaler halfway down his throat. 'He was investigating a sheep. Oh Fat!'

Gerard sat down again and drew his knees up to his chest, folding himself into the shape that Fat loved to use as a resting place. Would he ever nestle there again? Gerard lowered his head onto his knees and clasped his hands around them, so that the others wouldn't see his tears.

'Look, Gerard,' said Beverley, hunkering down beside him and whispering in his ear. 'We'll get Elizabeth to this house, and then you and I will come back here and look for Fat. He can't have gone far. This island isn't very big. He's probably up a tree or asleep on some nice sunny rock or something. When he gets hungry, he'll start looking for you. And we'll be there. We'll find him. OK?'

'OK,' said Gerard in an unsteady voice, but without raising his head. He didn't know what to make of all this unexpected tenderness from Beverley, but he was grateful for it all the same.

'Come on, so, Kevin,' said Beverley, making gestures to the others above Gerard's head not to tease him, to let him have his little weep. She bent down and laid her crossed arms on the ground.

'Cross your arms too, Kevin,' she ordered, 'and then grab my hands. Right. Now, Liz, wiggle your bottom onto our hands. Ouch! OK. And away we go! Heave-ho!'

Kevin and Beverley struggled to an upright position, with

Elizabeth still trying to balance herself between them.

'Nice view up here!' she announced, a good head and shoulders above her bearers, with her bad leg stuck out uncomfortably in front.

'Terrible view down here!' muttered Beverley, her head half buried under Elizabeth's armpit.

'Now, the secret is to march in step,' said Kevin. 'One, two, three, left, right, left.'

And so the strange caravan lumbered forward: Kevin and Beverley toiling and trying to co-ordinate their breathing as well as their footsteps; Elizabeth trying to will herself to be as light as possible, thinking aeroplane in flight, ballerina in a *sauté*, swallow on the wing, butterflies fluttering, gossamer in the breeze, dandelion-seed parachutes flitting through the air; and Gerard trailing disconsolately behind, dragging the garden flare, his face more streaked than ever, and calling out hopelessly 'Fat, Fat!' every now and then.

Chapter 13

THE HOUSE THAT WASN'T
MADE OF GINGERBREAD

BEVERLEY THOUGHT THE JOURNEY WOULD NEVER END. As well as being hot and sticky and tired, she could hardly see. Elizabeth's hair slid in a stifling, blinding, unpredictable curtain in front of Beverley's face, and sweat poured down her forehead and into her eyes. Her shoulders ached desperately, and she had to feel her way along carefully with her feet, in case she encountered a root or a stone or a hole in the path. All they needed now was for one of them to trip, and the whole pantomime camel of herself, Kevin and Elizabeth would go pitching headlong, maybe bringing down Gerard as well.

At last a muffled yell from Gerard reached Beverley's ears through Elizabeth's hair: 'I see the house. It's not far!'

'Ouch!' said Beverley. 'Don't!'

'Sorry,' came the reply from almost in her ear. Kevin's head was only a foot away, on the other side of Elizabeth. He'd tightened his grip on Beverley's wrists without meaning to.

'I – need – a – rest,' said Beverley.

'Right, so. Down we go.'

Gently, Beverley and Kevin lowered their burden onto the ground and sat down themselves too. As soon as her arms were free, Beverley flopped onto her back and her hands raised themselves, almost automatically, into the air in front of her. Pins and needles gushed exquisitely along her veins, as she waved her arms ecstatically over her head.

When at last she could feel her fingers, and could wriggle them all individually, one to ten, Beverley sat up. Elizabeth was examining her ankle again. It looked ghastly.

'Where's the house?' Beverley asked Gerard, who was the only member of the party still standing.

'Stand up,' he ordered, squinting and pointing.

When she stood up and followed the direction of Gerard's finger, she could just glimpse the house, less than a hundred yards away. It was only barely visible, behind a tangle of trees and overgrown shrubs. It looked quite sweet, if a bit untidy. A lilac tree held up huge blue cones as if to hide the gable end, and two laburnum trees standing companionable guard wept ringlets of gold onto the grass. Everything was overblown, reaching the end of its blossoming time, scattering petals and whole florets on the grassy earth. The chimney peered over the top of it all, as if the house were standing on tiptoe to get a better view of the pilgrim children.

'Right, well now, will we give it one last heave?' asked Kevin, talking to Beverley but looking up at the looming clouds with a worried expression on his face.

Beverley looked at the sky, which seemed very close to the earth now, and was heavy with purplish-grey clouds. There was going to be a lot of rain, the very wettest sort of rain. It made sense to get to the house before it started.

'All right,' she agreed, longing for rain to rinse away the weight at the heart of the afternoon, and yet dreading it, wanting to get to the shelter of the house, yet strangely apprehensive about it, as if Kevin's worries had transmitted themselves to her, in spite of herself. She hunkered down and crossed her arms again. Kevin grasped her hands firmly and Elizabeth worked her way with a practised wriggle onto the seat they made for her.

A climbing rose had grown right over the lichen-spattered gate pillars, its dense yellow heads bobbing stately, throwing their rich, sweet scent carelessly into the gathering air, but the gateway itself was free, with just a few thorny rose twigs wound around the hinges. Gerard creaked the wrought-iron gate open, and Kevin turned around and backed through at an angle, still gripping Beverley's hands tightly and with Elizabeth hanging on around his neck.

'Ouch!' yelped Elizabeth, as a thorn scraped her face. 'I'm all right,' she added, when her sedan chair stopped with a lurch. 'It's only a scratch.'

Meanwhile, Gerard had got to the front door. It was a stout old door, painted what might once have been a sky blue, but was now a blistering and peeling dirty grey. It was firmly shut. He knocked loudly, and the sound echoed in the children's ears.

No reply.

Good, thought Kevin. Maybe she was away. Maybe she'd stayed on the mainland. Sometimes she went to the bank.

Gerard knocked again, this time rapping more firmly and more often.

Still no reply. Gerard looked around at the others.

'Nobody home,' he said, stating the obvious. 'I'll see if I can get in around the back, and I'll open it from the inside, if I can.' He was already wading through fading London pride and flaming marigolds, which grew in fierce confusion around the sides of the house. He was still incongruously brandishing the tatty but intact garden flare.

Moments later, the front door creaked slowly inwards as if of its own accord, as if the house wasn't quite sure whether it wanted to admit this band of strangers. It must have made up its mind, however, for eventually it opened wide enough to admit the children.

'Thanks, Gerard!' called Elizabeth.

Kevin and Beverley stumbled in with Elizabeth between them. This time, Elizabeth cowered right down, in case anything nasty like a door lintel or a cobweb got her in the face.

The hallway was small, square and flagged. A rickety wooden staircase rose almost perpendicularly to what must be attic rooms. There was a door on the right and a door on the left. The children stood still, bunched together in the hall, and listened. Not a sound.

'Hello?' said Beverley, a tight, bright voice.

Nothing.

'What's that smell?' asked Beverley after a moment, sniffing the thick dank air of the hall.

Gerard gave a stifled sob of recognition.

'Cat!' said Elizabeth. 'I'd know that pong anywhere. Our car stinks of it.'

'Does it really?' asked Kevin, intrigued, in spite of himself, by this curious fact. 'Why?'

Elizabeth opened her mouth to tell him, but then she caught sight of Gerard's pinched and worried-looking little face, and a kindness came over her. She shut her mouth and said nothing.

Then she opened it again and said: 'Do you think you could let me down now? It's a bit wobbly up here.'

Beverley looked around the back of Elizabeth's head at Kevin, her eyebrows raised enquiringly. Kevin nodded. Now they'd got here, there was nothing for it but to see what this house had to offer in the way of food, shelter and running water.

'Kitchen!' ordered Kevin and started to back into the room on the left of the hall.

He was right in his choice. It was a dark kitchen, dark and cool, like a dairy or a pantry, only not as wholesome, with a lingering catty pong here too, overlaying an earthy smell that the children would have recognised as damp if they'd had more experience of old houses.

After their eyes had adjusted to the gloom, the children could see an old-fashioned sofa against one wall, the kind they have in psychiatrists' surgeries in films. It was covered in wine-coloured leatherette and there were only one or two holes in it, where the stuffing was coming out. It seemed to be stuffed with straw. Beverley and Kevin lowered Elizabeth onto the sofa with great relief.

The holes in the sofa looked dangerously like rats' nests, thought Beverley. Perhaps it was just as well there were cats after all. At least it meant there wouldn't be rats – or probably not anyway.

Elizabeth stretched out on the sofa and said: 'Thanks, you guys. You were great to carry me all that way.'

'Yes, we were, weren't we?' agreed Beverley, whose arms had started to do their levitation act again.

Kevin pulled a chair out. The crossbar at the back came away in his hand.

'We used to have a chair like that,' said Gerard.

'Like this? Moth-eaten?' asked Kevin, as he wrestled to re-insert the uprights into the crossbar.

'Moths don't eat chairs,' Beverley pointed out pedantically. 'It might have been woodworm, I suppose.'

'I mean, one that the back used to come off if you pulled at it.' Gerard went on helpfully: 'It's probably just that the glue has dried up. You just need to reglue it.'

'Well, do you know what?' said Kevin skittishly. 'I'm after forgetting to bring my pocket-pack of Uhu. Isn't that just terrible, now!'

Everyone tittered. Their nervous laughter echoed eerily around the empty kitchen. The children's gazes followed the half-hearted laughter, taking in the bleak little room. Like the house, the kitchen looked only half-derelict. Even the chair was only half-bockety.

There was an old oil-cloth on the square kitchen table. It had little orange flowers on it, like the montbretia you see growing wild at the seaside, only without the foliage. There were rings on the cloth, where somebody'd put a cup or mug down.

Beverley put out a disapproving finger and traced one of the rings. It was sticky. She looked at the gunge it created on her finger tip for some time before the significance of this struck her.

'This is a fresh ring,' she said loudly, waving her brown-tipped finger about excitedly.

The others looked at her blankly.

'I mean, somebody put a cup down here not too long ago. Or maybe it was a jar of honey or jam. Anyway, whoever lives here can't be far away.'

Beverley was moving around the room now. She put a tentative hand out to the range. It was stone cold. Well, it was June after all. There was a gas stove too. Also cold. Of course, gas stoves don't retain heat for long. Then she looked in the sink, which was brown with age. There were no taps, only a dangerous-looking contraption that might or might not be a pump. A mug with tea in the bottom sat in the middle of the sink, with a plate of crumbs tilting against it. There were streaks and blobs of honey on the plate too.

Beverley stuck her finger into the dregs of the tea. Not quite stone cold, but not what you could call warm. Luke-cold, she decided. Yes, somebody had definitely had tea not very long ago. The occupant of the house couldn't be far away.

The sash window over the sink, which was overgrown with some sort of climber, was thrown up to let the summer air in. The climber explained why it was so dark in here, that and the glowering clouds outside. Biggish chinks of grey-black clouds showed through the foliage curtain. Beverley peered out of the window, half-convinced she'd heard a shuffling sound outside.

'Hello,' said Beverley suddenly.

The others jumped, but it was only a very large cow that Beverley was talking to, a cow that was making her way towards the house, swaying her tail and making slow, wet, snuffling noises as she waded through the garden.

The cow looked lugubriously in at Beverley through the leafy curtain and made that hypnotic movement with her jaws that cows do, like a large, insolent, thoughtful child chewing gum.

'I suppose we could milk her if the worst comes to the worst,' came Elizabeth's voice from the sofa.

'Oh!' said Beverley. 'Yes, I suppose we could.' But she didn't like the idea. 'Kevin, do you know how?'

But Kevin didn't reply. He was sitting quietly in the half-bockety chair, wondering what to say if she came back, the witch, the madwoman, whatever she was, and found them all here, lolling about in her kitchen.

After a while, the cow turned away and started to munch the garden. The children sat and listened to the wet, munching sounds, and their tummies rumbled.

Chapter 14

WHO'S BEEN SITTING IN
MY CHAIR?

RIGHT, THOUGHT BEVERLEY, the thing now is to see to Elizabeth's foot. The whole expedition had been a bit of a disaster, she had to admit, and it was time just to cut their losses and make good their escape. But they couldn't do that with Elizabeth laid up. Somehow, they had to get the foot better – and quickly.

The sink was the best prospect, but Beverley couldn't see how they were going to get Elizabeth's foot into it. It wasn't so much the foot that was going to be the problem as what to do with the rest of Elizabeth while her foot was in the sink. Beverley was so absorbed in this problem that she didn't hear the footsteps outside in the garden.

Kevin heard them, though. He'd been straining and listening for this very sound ever since they'd arrived at the house. He thought he'd heard the faint click of the gate closing. It was the merest suggestion of a sound, but he was almost sure he'd heard it. Why hadn't he heard it screech open? Maybe they'd left it hanging open. Yes, yes he thought they had. The closing of the gate was followed by soft, shooshing steps, the sound of someone wading through lush grasses and wildflowers in the garden.

He swung a glance around the room. Elizabeth and Beverley

were apparently deep in consideration of Elizabeth's swollen ankle. But Gerard was sitting slightly apart and staring out of the window. At the sound of the footsteps, his head swivelled around and his eyes met Kevin's. Kevin could swear he'd heard it too, but neither boy spoke. They just held each other's stares and sat very, very still.

Now there was another sound. It was like humming. No, no, it wasn't humming. It was more like somebody talking. Or maybe it was sort of half-way between talking and singing. Yes, it was like someone murmuring, crooning, in the soft, sing-song tone a woman might use to her baby. She was talking, crooning to herself. She must be off her rocker.

The murmuring and the shooshing steps came nearer. Surely the girls must hear it now? But neither Elizabeth nor Beverley looked up. Kevin saw Gerard's eyes grow wide, but he willed the younger boy not to scream or flinch. Now there was a hand on the doorknob. It creaked in its socket and turned with a moan.

Oh my God! thought Kevin. I should never have let them come here. I should have put them all somewhere safe, in a cave or behind a sand-dune or something, and I should have swum back to the mainland for help. Except I can't swim. Oh, why did I never learn to swim?

The door inched open.

What sort of monster was going to appear, and what was she going to say to them? Would she have a wart on her nose and a pointy chin? Frantically, Kevin searched his memory. Had he ever actually seen the madwoman of Lady Island? He couldn't remember that he had. Would she have an evil black cat and a wicked wand? Would she shoo them all out of her house and threaten them with the law? Could you actually be sued for trespass anyway? Or would she take them hostage and blackmail their parents? Or fatten them up for her dinner? Nonsense, Kevin told himself, that was utter nonsense, but even so, an eerie, fearful feeling crept along his skin and made the little hairs on his arms shoot up like a hedgehog's quills.

The kitchen door opened fully, and in walked a stoutish woman in a beige raincoat tied around the middle with blue twine, and with a funny squashed-looking, battered brown velvet hat on her head. She had an off-white cat in her arms.

Gerard gave a yelp of surprise, dismay, terror and delight. Fat! He leapt to his feet, his arms outstretched. But he stopped short of actually wrenching the cat from the woman's arms, and stood, waiting for her to hand Fat over.

Beverley and Elizabeth looked up in surprise at the sound of Gerard's yelp and saw the woman. A hand flew to Beverley's mouth and clamped it shut. Screaming now would never do.

For a long time the woman didn't speak. She just stood there in the doorway in her three-quarter-length wellingtons – the tops had been hacked off – and stared at the children, as if drinking them all in. Another cat had followed her into the kitchen, waving its tail high in the air and lifting its paws daintily in an elegant dance in and out between her legs, over her wellington-booted feet. The woman seemed almost ordinary, apart maybe from the wellingtons and the blue twine. She looked at the children curiously, but she didn't seem surprised to see them. The four children stared back at the woman, silent, apprehensive, curious.

The only one who made any attempt at conversation was the cat in the woman's arms. He was purring loudly. He had his forepaws around the woman's neck in an unusually familiar gesture, and his head was stretched up to nuzzle her cheek, in a loving hug.

The silence stretched on, and still the woman stood and stared.

A thought struck Kevin. He leapt up, meaning to say, Would you like to sit down, Ma'am?, but although he opened his mouth and moved his tongue against his teeth and lips, no sound came out. But the woman understood his gesture and stepped forward to take the chair he was shoving forward. Kevin was so eager to seat this strange hostess in her own house that he gave the chair too strong a push in her direction, and the crossbar came away again in his hand. 'Sorry,' he muttered, and tried to fix it back in place, but he couldn't seem to manage it. The more he shoved, the less able he seemed to fit the chair back together. In desperation, Kevin pushed at it too hard, and one of the uprights forming the back came out as well and rattled to the floor. Kevin looked up to see how the woman was taking all this.

She was just standing there, coolly watching him. Suddenly she tumbled the cat out of her arms and took off her funny old hat, to reveal surprisingly youthful chestnut hair, which she shook out with some pride. As soon as the cat turned around to land gracefully on his feet, Gerard saw that it wasn't Fat. It was a longer, thinner, taller cat, but with the same dirty-cream fur. Disappointment wrenched at him and made his eyes prickle and his throat ache.

The woman put her hat on the table and then she said in a high-pitched, stagey voice: '*Who's* been sitting in *my* chair?'

For a moment nobody breathed a sound. Then, as if at a signal, the four children all laughed, a short, experimental sort of laugh. Then they laughed a bit more. They laughed and laughed. Their laughter became hysterical. They doubled over with laughter and tears flowed down their cheeks. It wasn't all that funny, really, but somehow it was as if they couldn't stop laughing. Miraculously, the woman laughed with them.

When his laughter had finally settled into sporadic, gusty sobs,

Kevin fixed first the upright and then the crossbar into place, and then offered the chair again. The woman came forward and sat down. For a moment there was another fraught silence.

'You're a Mulrooney, from the shop at Tranarone,' said the woman at last, to Kevin, in an ordinary sort of voice, not the squeaky baby-bear voice she'd used earlier.

What a relief! thought Beverley. What an ordinary thing to say! Maybe she wasn't anyone to be scared of after all. Well, for goodness' sake, what had they expected? A witch? Hardly! How could she be? What nonsense!

'Yes,' agreed Kevin. 'Kevin. I'm the oldest.'

'Ah, yes, Kevin,' said the woman. 'I knew your father, before he – well, in the old days. I know your poor mother too, of course.'

Kevin smiled faintly in acknowledgement of the family acquaintance, but he said nothing more.

Again, silence filled the kitchen, broken only by the cats' continuous purring. Beverley started to fidget. Kevin looked ill at ease again. Elizabeth was pale with pain or apprehension. Gerard looked distraught. Only the woman seemed unperturbed by the situation.

'Well,' she said at last, to everyone's relief, and, looking at Beverley for some unexplained reason, she went on: 'You might at least put the kettle on.'

The kettle! That meant tea. There might even be bread and butter, or biscuits. In spite of themselves, the children perked up at the thought, though they didn't dare to show their eagerness for food – not so much out of politeness, but out of something more like wariness. The woman seemed friendly enough, but they didn't want to push their luck.

Beverley jumped up and ran to the sink, snatching the dirt-encrusted kettle from the stove as she passed. Confronted by the strange-looking contraption that might or might not be a pump, she touched it speculatively, wondering what to do.

'It's a pump,' said the woman. 'You have to work the handle up and down.'

'Oh, I see,' said Beverley. Really, she was perfectly ordinary, a perfectly ordinary woman. Nothing to be afraid of, Beverley told herself.

Beverley applied some strength to the pump handle, and sure enough on the second or third pull the water came rushing out, straight onto the dishes in the sink, which made it splash back up and all over Beverley's clothes. She flinched, and then moved the dishes aside and placed the kettle in the stream of water. It filled with a musical gush. With shaking hands, Beverley took the kettle to the stove.

'Matches!' she hissed at Elizabeth, who had to wriggle to get them out of her pocket. The gas lit with a smelly blue fizz, and Beverley put the kettle carefully on top of it. All the while, the woman watched her intently, not saying a thing.

When she'd finished, Beverley stood with her hands behind her back, as if waiting for more orders. She wondered if they should apologise for being here, or explain. But their hostess didn't look the sort who expected or wanted apologies.

'The cups are on the dresser,' said the woman, who seemed to be enjoying having someone to order around. 'And there's a few packets of shortbread under the dresser. And honey. I'll have honey with mine. I'm afraid that's all I can offer you, though, I'm out of food.'

Out of food? thought Kevin. How could she be out of food? He'd delivered her groceries to the pier that morning, and there'd been powdered milk, sardines, baked beans, fresh vegetables and fruit, packets of soup, custard powder – any amount of food. There'd been shortbread too, of course, and loads of honey. There always was.

'Hell's bells!' said Beverley under her breath, peering into the cupboard that formed the lower part of the kitchen dresser. It was stuffed with packet upon packet of shortbread, and there were pots and pots of honey, and nothing else. But she didn't comment, just brought the things to the table and laid them out – the shortbread, the honey, a cup with the Indian tree design on it and a chip out of the goldy bit at the top of the handle, two blue-band mugs that were a bit brown on the inside, a mug that said I'm the Boss in large bold letters and was crazed on the inside, an empty honey jar to do for a fifth cup, a teapot without a lid, a yoghurt carton half full of sugar and with a sugar-encrusted spoon sticking out of it, and the tea-caddy, which had some partially rusted red roses on it.

'I can't find any milk,' she said apologetically.

'There isn't any,' said the woman. 'I'm always running out of milk.'

'No milk?' asked Beverley. 'But what about the cow?'

'Oh, she doesn't mind,' said the woman. 'She doesn't drink tea.'

'No,' said Beverley, suppressing a smile, 'I mean, do you not milk her?'

'Certainly not!' said the woman in a shocked voice.

'This is like a proper pilgrimage,' said Elizabeth happily. 'Black tea is just perfect.'

There she went again, with her blessed pilgrimage!

'So, who's going first?' asked the woman unexpectedly, as she lined the cups up in a neat row on the table.

The children started. Going? So she wasn't friendly after all!

She wanted them to go! They looked sadly at the little tea-party laid out on the table and they thought about how hungry they were. But they thought they'd better get out of here before she turned nasty.

'We'll all go together,' Gerard spurted out.

'No, no, I don't mean that,' said the woman, waving her hand in a sit-down-and-don't-be-annoying-me gesture. 'I mean with the story. Who's going first with the story?'

Elizabeth gulped. How did this woman know about the stories?

'What story?' she asked, in a small, shaky voice.

'Your story,' said the woman.

'I've already told mine,' countered Elizabeth.

'Yes,' she said mysteriously. 'Yes, that's right.'

In a flash, Elizabeth remembered a sneeze on the beach. A sneeze none of *them* had sneezed. She remembered a snort too. She'd thought it had been the sheep. And she remembered an eerie sense she'd felt all day that someone was watching them and listening to them. Surely the woman hadn't been sneaking around and spying on them? Elizabeth shifted uneasily on her sofa. What exactly was going on here? And how come the woman was so keen to hear a story? Was she some sort of collector of stories, or what?

'It's my turn,' said Beverley, jumping in bravely. 'I'll tell.'

'Oh good,' said the woman. 'But first, the tea.' And she reached out, opened the teacaddy and tipped a large quantity of fine black tea into the lidless teapot. Then she gestured to Beverley to pour hot water on it, and, when it was filled, she plonked the honey jar on top, instead of a lid. 'Keeps the steam in *and* melts the honey,' she remarked to no-one in particular.

'So it does!' agreed Gerard, smiling at the woman's simple cleverness. She smiled back, a wide, warm smile, or so he thought at any rate.

Chapter 15

BEVERLEY'S TALE

'ONCE THERE WAS A BEAUTIFUL YOUNG GIRL with long legs and wonderful long golden hair,' Beverley began, after everyone had got steaming cups of hot red tea and thick fingers of shortbread, dripping with honey.

'No, no,' the woman interrupted. 'That can't be right. Stumpy little legs and wiry black hair, I think would be a more accurate description.'

Beverley didn't quite know how to respond to this. She wondered if she should humour the woman, to be on the safe side, or whether she should just tell the story her way. She thought for a few moments and then said: 'No. This girl had long slim legs and long golden hair.'

'Well, it can't be the same girl then,' said the woman, sounding satisfied with her own explanation.

'Maybe not,' agreed Beverley warily. 'Anyway, this beautiful girl –'

'But in that case,' went on the woman, 'I think you must be telling the wrong story. I want to hear *your* story.'

'This *is* my story,' said Beverley.

'Are you sure?'

'Of course I'm sure. I'm telling it, aren't I?'

'Hmm.' The woman didn't seem convinced.

'So anyway, this beautiful young girl lived deep in the forest.'

'What forest?' asked the woman.

'Just a forest,' said Beverley.

'But there aren't any forests hereabouts.'

'It wasn't hereabouts.'

'I don't think I understand this story at all,' sighed the woman.

'You don't have to understand it,' said Beverley with sudden authority. Now that she was telling a story, she felt in charge of things again. 'You just have to listen. And don't ask so many questions. It only confuses the issue.' She surprised herself by sounding so positive, but she had an irresistible urge to shut the woman up and get on with the story. She felt almost compelled to tell it.

'On the contrary,' said the woman. 'I usually find that asking questions clarifies the issue. That is,' she added slyly, 'if I get helpful answers.'

'Well, this is the sort of story you just have to listen to,' said Beverley firmly, 'and not ask questions about. Except,' she relented, 'at the end. Maybe.'

'All right,' the woman said agreeably, stirring a *fifth* spoon of sugar into her tea – Beverley didn't mean to count, but she couldn't help it. 'Carry on so.'

'Now the reason she lived so deep in this dense forest is that a fairy had predicted at her birth that her son would slay her father. Do you see what I mean?' Beverley asked kindly, thinking she'd better make sure her audience was following her, as she'd forbidden questions.

'Yes, yes,' said the woman. 'I'm not stupid. Someone told this lassie's father that he'd better not let his daughter get married, or

134

even within a sniff of a husband, just to be on the safe side, because if she did, and if she had a son, then the young fellow would one day kill his grandfather. So presumably Papa decides to hide the daughter away where she is in no danger of marrying anyone and having a son and that way he thinks he's going to be safe. Is that right?'

'Exactly,' said Beverley.

'Happens in all the best stories,' said the woman. 'But to be honest, I find it all a bit far-fetched.'

'So,' Beverley continued, ignoring the woman's comment, 'as well as hiding his daughter away in the depths of this forest, the father cast a spell, and the spell was that any young man who came to visit his daughter would have to undergo a test before being allowed even to see her, much less marry her. If he failed the test, the father would slice off his head, and the young man would turn into a pine tree. That's where the forest had come from. Every tree in that forest represented a suitor that the girl had had. But even though the evidence of failure was plain to see in the shape of the dense, dark forest, young men continued to come and try for the hand of this beautiful young girl. One by one they failed the test the girl's father put to them, and one by one they were beheaded and turned into trees.

'The father's plan was working out very satisfactorily, he decided. His daughter was safe from prying eyes in the middle of the forest, and any prospective husband who came even as far as the edge of the forest was soon turned into a pine tree, for none of them could ever pass the test.'

'What was the test?' asked Kevin.

'Well, that was the clever thing, you see. It was unpassable. Each young man was asked to chop down a pine tree and to carve a golden goblet out of the wood. And of course nobody could carve wood into gold, so each young man, on hearing what the task was, sadly had to admit that he couldn't perform it, and was immediately executed and turned into yet another pine tree, making it even more difficult for the next person who came along to penetrate the forest and see the beautiful girl hidden at its centre, like a jewel in a dark casket.'

'But that's not fair,' said Kevin. 'Sure it's impossible to do that!'

'Of course it's not fair,' said Beverley indignantly. 'You don't expect the man would have set a fair task, do you? That way somebody might have accomplished it.'

'Hmm,' said Kevin thoughtfully.

'Well, then, one day, a tall dark prince came riding into the forest. He didn't stop at the edge of the forest like all the others. He just rode boldly through the youngest pine trees on the outskirts of the forest and went riding on, more and more slowly, his progress impeded by the dense growth of green-dark trees.

'When the father got to hear of this bold young man riding through his forest, he immediately sent one of his slaves to accost the prince and tell him that he must either turn back immediately or face the task.

'Well, the young prince didn't hesitate for a moment when he heard the story of the impossible task and the hidden princess and he immediately agreed to hear what the task was and to attempt it.

'The slave warned him that once he had heard what the task was, the young man was obliged either to accomplish it or to submit to summary execution. Laughing at the absurdity of an impossible task, the prince instantly agreed to the challenge.

'Sadly, the slave told him that he would have to cut down a pine tree and carve a golden goblet from its wood. Upon hearing this, the young man lashed out with his sword and felled the nearest tree with ease, without even dismounting from his horse.

'Then, bending down lazily, he sliced the felled trunk into several large chunks, and then he picked up one of these and effortlessly started to whittle at it with his pocket knife, still seated in his saddle, and chattering pleasantly all the while to the wretched slave, who could see nothing but death and destruction in store for this young hero.

'As he worked the wood, the sap flew out from under the prince's knife in all directions, like a soft shower of piney-scented rain, and gradually the wood took on the shape of a most elegantly carved goblet. The young man worked on, shaping and whittling, until the goblet was finished, its surface gleaming and shining in the dense dark of the forest. Finally the prince put his pocket knife in his belt and took out a large handkerchief. This he used to polish and buff the pine goblet until its surface was perfectly smooth and silken to the fingertips. At last he was satisfied with his handiwork and he held the wooden goblet up in the air triumphantly and said: "There! A golden goblet, as requested." And he bowed deeply from the waist and handed the carved vessel to the slave.

'"But this is a wooden goblet," said the slave.

'"Indeed it is," agreed the young man.

'"The task was to carve a golden goblet," the slave said, thinking that this was rather a stupid fellow, for all his good looks and his happy chatter and his skill with his knife.

'"And what colour is this goblet?" asked the prince.

'"Why, it's golden," said the slave, gasping at the cleverness of the young man.

'"Precisely," said the young man, "it's golden. I think you asked me to fashion a golden goblet from the wood of this tree?"

'"Yes, but ..." spluttered the slave, certain he would be in deep trouble with his master over this, although he knew it wasn't his fault. "But it's not a goblet *of* gold," the slave managed to argue at last.

'"Well, of course it isn't of gold. It's of wood. Nevertheless, I contend that it is a golden goblet. Take it to your master and put this argument to him."

'The slave shook his head. He fingered the wonderful goblet, and he had to admit that it was undoubtedly of the richest gleaming golden colour he had ever seen, and it was warmer than gold to the touch, and sweeter than gold to the nose, and it received the light far more subtly than any gold. Still, he shook his head, but he agreed to approach his master with the goblet.

'The young man sat quietly on his horse, waiting for the slave to return, certain that his goblet would be accepted in fulfilment of the task he had been set. And indeed it was. The father of the girl didn't want to accept it of course, and he consulted long and hard with all his sorcerers and magicians, but they all advised him that the way he had cast the spell had left this loophole in the conditions, and there was no way that he could undo this now, and so he was forced by the terms of his own spell to accept the young man as a son-in-law.

'The slave came trotting merrily back through the forest with the news, delighted that this young man wasn't going to be beheaded and turned into a tree, for he had become rather fond of him, charmed by his gaiety, his confidence, his self-assurance and his certainty that he could outwit the father of the girl.

'Now that the father's first defence of his daughter – the forest

138

– had been penetrated, by this impudent stranger, and his second defence – the spell – had been broken, the father was forced to try other means to preserve his daughter from the man who was determined to have her hand. So while the slave was returning to the prince, he set about hiding his daughter more effectively. He used another spell to create a pit, deep in the heart of the forest, and into this pit he cast the princess, where nobody could reach her. He didn't use locks to lock her in; nor did he set dragons or mastiffs at the doorway; nor yet did he fill the pit with snakes nor surround it with fire. He didn't need any of these deterrents. He relied instead on the depth of the pit and its slimy, sheer walls which none could scale. Even if the young man could succeed in reaching the princess, it would be of no use to him, for there was certainly no way that the couple would ever be able to get out of the pit.

'When he heard what the father had done, the young man simply shrugged his shoulders and rode on slowly through the branchy forest, until he reached its very centre.

'He looked over the edge of the pit, but he could see nothing but pitch blackness. He shrugged again, clicked his teeth at his horse, and with that the horse rose up into the air, unfurling wings of gossamer as it leapt. When the wings were fully stretched, the horse and its rider hung for a moment in the air, and then they began to sink gently into the depths of the pit, the horse's elegant wings filling slowly with air and billowing about them like a parachute.

'At the bottom of the pit the golden-haired maiden sat shivering. Imagine her amazement when a magic horse landed beside her, with a tall and merry-looking fellow on its back.

'The prince explained that he had come to rescue her, and the princess was glad to hear it, for she had been trying in vain to gain a foothold on the slithery walls of the pit, and was beginning to despair of ever getting free.

'So the prince leant over and hauled the princess onto the horse's back with him, and together they sailed up into the air and right over the edge of the pit. When they got to the top of the pit, the horse still flew up and up, till he was high above the pit and high above the pine tops and high above the forest. On and on they flew towards the horizon, the princess's golden hair streaming out behind her, and her laughs of delight hanging in the air like frozen musical notes.

'When they arrived in the prince's country, the horse sank gracefully to earth and the prince and princess were able to dismount.

'"Thank you," said the young woman, sweeping her hair back over her shoulders and tying it up with a ribbon. "And now can you take me to a school for young ladies, or to a convent perhaps, or to a family where there is a mother who longs for a daughter as I have longed all my life for a mother?"

'"I will take you to my mother, the queen, and you can live with her for the time being, and make your preparations for the wedding," said the prince.

'"Is somebody getting married?" asked the princess.

'"Why, we are, of course," said the prince. "I accomplished the task your father set, in return for which I am entitled to your hand in marriage, and furthermore I have rescued you from the black pit where you were imprisoned."

'"But I have no wish to marry you," said the princess. "I am very grateful that you rescued me, but when you think about it, it was really your horse's flying power that rescued me. I am grateful also to your horse – it is a fine beast – but that doesn't mean I would want to marry it. And I would as soon marry you as marry your horse."

'"Marry my horse!" exclaimed the prince, outraged. "What sort of a princess would want to marry a horse?"

'"No, no. You misunderstand me," said the princess sweetly. "I mean that I do *not* want to marry either you or the horse, but that if I were obliged to marry my rescuer – which I am not – it is the horse who would have the first claim."

'"But what about the task?" argued the prince. "I fulfilled the task your father set, though no other man succeeded in it." And he told the princess the full story of the golden goblet of wood.

'The princess sat on a boulder to listen, and she twirled her hair around her finger as she listened. At last she spoke: "In the first place, though you did comply with the terms of the task as set, you know perfectly well that you only managed to achieve this by a trick of words. Secondly, and more important, in undertaking and fulfilling this task, you were entering into a contract not with me but with my father. I am sorry that my father should have promised my hand in marriage to whoever should accomplish this ridiculous task, but he never consulted me about it, and I contend that the agreement, though binding on him, is not binding on me, and since I am the one to be married, the agreement is thus annulled."

'When he heard this, the prince knew he had met his match for sure in this one. She was as clever as he, and as quick-witted, and more than ever he desired to marry her. But he saw that this princess was not to be won by trickery, nor by gallantry, nor through contractual arrangements made with her father.

'"I accede," he said graciously, mounting his horse. "If you do not wish to marry me, of course I will have to abide by your wishes. And now I will take you to my mother's house, and there you may live as long as you wish, and I will not trouble you again."

And he held out his hand to help her to mount also.

'"Thank you," said the princess for the second time, and hopped up lightly on the horse again, and with that the horse rose up in the air again and flew off to the prince's mother's house.'

Beverley stopped abruptly.

'Is that it?' asked Elizabeth, unconsciously twirling her hair about her fingers.

'Yes,' said Beverley.

'But did she marry him or not?'

'Oh, I don't know,' said Beverley airily. 'Perhaps. Perhaps not. Anyway, she's too young to be married. People in stories get married far too young. Maybe she will one day.'

'Aww!' said Elizabeth. 'I wish you'd tell us how it ends, Beverley.'

'Well, you didn't like the way Gerard's story ended, and you wanted to change it. And now I offer you a story to which you can tack on your own ending, and you're not happy with that either. You are not very logical, Elizabeth.'

Elizabeth knew she wasn't being logical, but she didn't think that logical was the thing to be in a case like this. She couldn't think of a way to explain that to Beverley, though. Beverley approved of logic above all things. Maybe that was why Elizabeth got such a strange feeling from her story. It was so unlike Beverley to leave a loose end like that. What could have got into her?

Chapter 16

THE BOTTLE LABELLED
LOTION

'I'M DYMPHNA,' SAID THE WOMAN SUDDENLY, offering a long brown hand to Gerard.

Beverley felt a bit put out that the strange woman hadn't mentioned how good her story was. Personally, she thought it was an amazing story, though to be honest, she had no idea where it came from. How on earth had she thought up that delightful play on the word 'golden'? And what was she doing anyway telling stories at a time like this? Here they were, stranded on this wretched island with an invalid on their hands and nobody knew where they were. Really, it wasn't like her to be so frivolous.

Gerard responded to the woman's introduction: 'Gerard,' he replied, grasping the woman's cool hand in his own sticky fist.

Not to be outdone, Beverley announced busily: 'And I'm Beverley. Kevin you seem to know. And that's Elizabeth with the foot.' Good heavens, the foot! she thought. We forgot all about bathing Elizabeth's foot.

They felt a bit peculiar introducing themselves at this stage, having been sitting together for some time, but Dymphna shook hands gravely with each one in turn, except Elizabeth, who was too far away.

'Has she got something wrong with her foot?' she asked, turning to look at the patient.

'Yes,' replied Elizabeth. 'I twisted my ankle.'

'That explains why she's lying down,' said the woman, as if they needed telling.

'That's mainly why we're here, actually,' said Beverley, surprised to be having such a sane conversation with their strange hostess. 'We wanted to bathe it, to reduce the swelling.'

'Oh, bathing it won't do much good,' said Dymphna airily. 'That well has lost its powers.'

The children looked mystified.

'But I might have a lotion,' she went on. 'I'll see after I have some more tea. Would you make a fresh pot, please, Gerard?'

'Honey, anyone?' she asked, waving the honey-pot around the tea-table, as Gerard scuttled about, making more tea.

'Are you the lady?' asked Gerard, when he'd made and poured more tea for everyone.

'Of the house, you mean?' asked Dymphna.

'No, of the island,' said Gerard.

'Lady of the island? Sounds like a poem. As in landlady, do you mean? I'm not, more's the pity. I'm here on sufferance, as you might say.'

The children wouldn't say any such thing. None of them knew what sufferance meant, but it sounded unpleasant.

'No, I mean as in "Lady Island",' said Gerard. 'That's what it's called, isn't it? Are you that lady?'

Dymphna fluffed her hair up with her rather elegant brown hands and laughed out loud.

'Arrah, of course she isn't,' Kevin cut in. 'This has been called Lady Island for centuries. She isn't centuries old.'

'How do you know how old I am?' asked Dymphna curiously and with a bit of a crotchety edge to her voice.

'Oh, excuse me,' said Kevin. 'I just mean, it's obvious you're not hundreds of years old.'

'What makes you think that?' Dymphna persisted, and with just a hint of hostility.

Kevin considered for a moment. 'History,' he said at last.

'Ah,' replied Dymphna, apparently satisfied with this answer.

Kevin gave a silent sigh of relief.

'So who is this lady then?' Gerard persisted.

Kevin was just about to explain about the seals and the mermaids, but Dymphna spoke first: 'That's *Our* Lady. As in the Madonna, you know, the BVM.'

Gerard didn't know, not really. He'd heard of Our Lady, of course, but he couldn't make any connection between her and Madonna, and he had no idea what BVM stood for, unless it was some sort of expensive car. He wasn't the sort of boy who bothered much with cars. But he nodded anyway, just to be polite.

'The island used to be a place of pilgrimage,' Dymphna went on. 'In the old days. Before that shower bought it. I don't think islands should be bought, do you? I think islands belong to God.'

'There, I *knew* it!' exclaimed Elizabeth, triumphantly. 'I said it all along. I said it was a pilgrimage.'

'Some of the old people from the mainland still come here on special feastdays. There's a holy well. It's supposed to cure you if you bathe in its waters. People used to leave their crutches behind, to prove they'd been cured. And bandages hanging out of the trees. And slings, things like that.'

'Doesn't sound very environment-friendly,' sniffed Beverley. 'Littering the place with bandages and things.'

'Oh don't say that!' cried Elizabeth. 'I think it's a lovely idea.'

'It's a lot of superstitious nonsense,' said Dymphna flatly. 'Either that or the water has lost its powers. It never cures *me* of anything anyway, and I have it pumped to my sink. I should be a model of good health if there's any truth in it. And I'm not. I get terrible arthritis and I have a chest. Did you leave your crutches?' The last bit was addressed to Elizabeth.

'No, I haven't got any crutches,' said Elizabeth. 'I only twisted my ankle this afternoon.'

'But why are you here then?' Again there was a hint of menace in the question, or so Beverley thought.

'We wanted to bathe the foot to reduce the swelling,' said Elizabeth. 'That's all. We didn't mean to intrude.'

'But I *told* you, it won't work.' Dymphna sounded emphatic, gruff even.

'I think it should,' said Beverley, who never knew when to keep quiet and not annoy people. 'Cold running water should at least help. And after we've bathed it, we should really bandage it up.'

She looked around, wondering what she could use as a bandage. It crossed her mind to ask Dymphna for an old sheet or tea-towel or something they could tear up, but she thought anything this woman would have was unlikely to be hygienic. Also, she wasn't sure how friendly Dymphna was. Better not give her a chance to be antagonistic.

'If we were in a *story*,' said Elizabeth dreamily, 'we'd be wearing petticoats, which we could valiantly tear into strips for bandages.'

'Only if it was a very *old* story,' said Beverley doubtfully. 'Girls haven't worn petticoats for yonks. And not with jeans anyway.'

'Would my shirt sleeves be any good to ye?' suggested Kevin.

'I could cut them off and wear the shirt like a vest, a jerkin, you know.'

'Ooh – black bandages!' said Elizabeth with distaste.

'Can't afford to turn your nose up, can you, Liz?' said Beverley pragmatically. 'OK, Kevin, take it off.'

'What's happening?' asked Dymphna, through a mouthful of shortbread and honey.

'Kevin's taking off his shirt to make a bandage for Elizabeth,' Gerard explained.

'Oh no, wait,' said Dymphna. 'First the lotion. Will you get it for me, Gerard? It's upstairs in the bedroom – that's in the attic, the stairs from the hall goes right up into it. It'll be under the bed, in a big trunk. It's in a bottle labelled "Lotion", and it's pink.'

'Labelled just "Lotion"?'

'Yes, of course. What else would I label it? "Whiskey"? "Paraffin Oil"? It's lotion, so naturally I label it "Lotion". That makes sense, doesn't it?'

Gerard couldn't quite put his finger on the flaw in this argument. He looked at Dymphna thoughtfully. At least, he felt thoughtful, but to Dymphna, his face merely looked blank.

'Oh look,' she said, 'it doesn't matter. I'll go for it myself. I'll just be two ticks.' And she disappeared so fast, in a flurry of furry tails and mews, the children could almost have sworn she flew out of the room, accompanied by two flying cats.

As soon as the door had closed on Dymphna, a silence settled on the children. They looked at each other, but nobody uttered a sound. It was as if each one was afraid to say what he or she was thinking, in case the others agreed. At last Elizabeth said tentatively: 'She's a bit weird, isn't she?'

'Mmm,' said Beverley uneasily.

'No, she's not,' said Gerard hotly. 'She's nice and kind and funny. And she likes cats.'

'Funny, yes, I grant you, she's definitely funny all right,' said Beverley. She was filling an old enamel basin she had found, to bathe Elizabeth's foot. She'd given up on the sink idea. 'Here, put your foot in this, Liz.'

The water was ice-cold. Elizabeth winced as she lowered her foot into it, which Beverley took to be a good sign.

'She's not funny in that horrible way you mean,' said Gerard. 'Her problem is, she's just too sensible for the rest of us. She just makes too much sense, that's all.'

'No, it's not just that,' said Elizabeth, lifting her foot gingerly out of the basin and letting the water drip off it in a little silvery shower. 'She's weird all right. I think this island is enchanted, and *she's* the enchantress. She enchants people to make them tell stories, and she listens to them, because she's a story-gatherer. Maybe she *steals* them!'

'Leave your foot in it, Elizabeth,' ordered Beverley. 'The cold will do it good. And there's no such thing as an enchantress.'

'Ouch!' said Elizabeth grumpily, but obediently put her foot back in the basin and kept it there until the water became almost luke-warm from the heat of her flesh. 'But it's a lovely word, isn't it?' she added, inconsequentially.

'I think we should just try to get this foot fixed as fast as we can,' Beverley went on, 'and get out of here.'

'I wouldn't think she's *dangerous*,' said Kevin slowly, as if trying to convince himself.

'Dangerous! Jeez, I never thought of dangerous!' said Elizabeth.

Suddenly there came from somewhere over their heads a wild,

eerie wail, an inhuman sound, like a mad cat, or a wolf baying at the moon. The sound hung in the air for what seemed like minutes and a shiver seemed to run around the room, passing quickly through each of the children and on to the next person. Gradually the sound petered away, like a siren running out of steam, and as it did, the shiver died down too. The children looked at each other sheepishly, each one wondering if it had really happened or if they had imagined it.

'I said I thought she *wasn't* dangerous,' said Kevin, gingerly picking up the conversation that had been interrupted by the wailing, but not sounding so convinced any more.

'Of course she's not dangerous!' Gerard broke in angrily. 'And she's not weird either. She's cool.'

The sound came again, almost as if to contradict him. This time it seemed to be more high-pitched than before, and this time they knew it was for real, because they could see the fear in each other's faces. Even Gerard's face was white and his mouth had fallen open with fright.

The children moved uneasily.

'We have to get out of here,' Beverley said as the sound died down. 'She's mad.'

'How do you know it's her?' asked Gerard, though he knew it must be. 'Maybe it's one of the cats.'

'That's no cat,' said Elizabeth.

'She's mad, I tell you,' said Beverley. 'I mean, why on earth does she live out here, all by herself? No, she's mad all right. I hope she's not bad too.'

The sound came again, and this time there was a terrible sadness in it as well as terror and madness. It was like the sound a person in great anguish would make. The children felt strange aching feelings in their throats, as though they wanted to cry.

'I think it's coming from *outside* the house,' Beverley whispered.

'I think you're right,' said Kevin and he tiptoed to the door and slipped out of the house. The others looked at one another in dismay. Now what was going on? Beverley had a moment of panic. What if Kevin didn't come back? What if he left them here with this deranged person? How was she going to cope? How was she going to protect the two younger ones? And how on earth was she going to get them all off this island? She had a sudden longing for her parents and a very clear conviction that she didn't want to be the oldest. If Kevin abandoned them, she would be (not counting the crazy woman), which meant she'd have to be in charge. How could she ever have wanted to be in charge? Being in charge was awful!

To Beverley's intense relief, Kevin was back in a moment, and as he reappeared, the wailing moved down a key and began to trail off into a long, quiet moan.

'She's standing at the upstairs window,' Kevin whispered. 'The window is wide open and she's sort of half hanging out of it and she's just wailing at the sky.'

Again the shiver shot around the group, bringing up a quick crop of goosebumps as it flew.

'Baying at the moon,' said Beverley, 'like a lunatic.'

'But it's the afternoon,' Kevin pointed out. 'There's no moon.'

'Well, that just makes her even madder,' said Beverley. 'Normal lunatics only go mad at the full moon.'

'She's *not* mad,' said Gerard fiercely. 'She's just, maybe, a bit *upset*.'

'What would upset her enough for that sort of –?' Beverley

began, but she didn't get to finish her question, because at that moment, there was a series of bumps and lurches in the hall, and the children all fell silent again as Dymphna came hurtling in the door, accompanied by her tail-swirling cats. The children found themselves shrinking back and putting their arms up in front of their faces, as if expecting her to attack them, but she didn't. Instead, she waved a very large bottle, three-quarters full of a pale pink liquid and labelled, in firm black handwriting on a browning old label, "Lotion".

'Hah!' said Dymphna, her eyes blazing, and set the bottle down on the table with a thud. 'I *knew* it was there.' She sounded defiant, as if the children had insisted there was no lotion and she had proved them wrong.

Nobody said a word. They lowered their arms sheepishly and looked uneasily at the floor, the ceiling, the bottle of lotion, anywhere rather than look her in the eye, though she swivelled her gaze from one to the other as if looking for someone to pick on.

'What's wrong?' she asked. 'You all look as if you've seen a ghost.'

'Oh no!' said Beverley quickly. 'We haven't seen anything, honest.'

'Or maybe you *heard* something?' Dymphna persisted, her eyes boring into Beverley. 'Is that what it is? Did you? Did you?'

'N-no!' said Beverley. 'Only the wind, I think.'

'Ah yes,' said Dymphna. 'The wind is getting up all right. Yes, yes, it must be It is, yes, it's the wind. Whoooo-oooo! Whooo-ooooo!' And with that she lifted the hem of her raincoat on each side with the tips of her middle fingers, like a little girl in a puffy dress, and held the fabric away from her body and did a little twirl, still singing 'Whooo-whooo!' She twirled again, 'Whooo-whoooo!' and again and again, faster and faster.

The children watched her in amazement as she whirled around her kitchen, whoo-ing and dancing, her feet flying round and round in her wellington boots, her long hair whipping the air around her face and shoulders. Then suddenly a calm seemed to descend on her, and she sat down abruptly at the table, pulled her hair back from her steaming red face, gathered one of the cats onto her knee and began to rock back and forth, crooning gently to the cat and ignoring the children.

Chapter 17

THE STORM

THE CHILDREN SAT AS IF TRANSFIXED, not knowing what to do, waiting for Dymphna to make the next move. The wind really was getting up now, almost as if her wild dance had been a wind-dance, calling up the wind from the corners of the earth. The foliage at the window started to rattle, beating against the pane, the leaves fluttering into the kitchen, and the murky light in the little room started to thicken until it was almost like evening. The children still sat, thinking their thoughts, and looming at each other in the gloom. Kevin was running his hands repeatedly through his hair, as if he was trying to come up with some sort of plan to get away from Dymphna and her madness and this eerie little house and the whole damned bewitched island.

'Storm coming,' said Dymphna suddenly, tilting her knees complacently so that the cat fell right off her lap and landed with a yelp of surprise on the floor.

She stood up and strode to the window, shoving it up with a practised wrist. Then she turned to a drawer and withdrew a wodge of cotton wool and a spool of Sellotape. With this equipment she started to create a sort of bandage for a small hole in the upper pane. She stuffed it first with cotton wool and then plastered it over several times with Sellotape. The children watched her in silence. They could see old bits of Sellotape hanging from it, trailing wisps of yellowing cotton wool. Evidently such bandaging went on regularly.

Then Dymphna left the kitchen. They could all hear her opening the front door and calling out: 'Dymphna, Dymphna!'

The four children exchanged glances. Talking to yourself was one thing, wailing at the sky and doing wind-dances in your kitchen was another, but calling yourself in out of the rain took the biscuit for daftness!

They could hear a shuffling, snuffling noise, which seemed to come in response to Dymphna's call, and a muffled moo in the hall. Good grief! It must be the cow! Then came another, lighter, more plaintive moo.

The children could hear Dymphna talking some more, in soft tones of endearment, and then another door, somewhere else in the house, opened and, after more snuffles and scuffles, closed.

'Just bringing Dymphna in out of the storm,' said Dymphna, coming back into the kitchen. 'She hates getting wet.' Her voice was matter-of-fact, utterly sane. She could have been the village shopkeeper or the parish priest's housekeeper talking about her favourite old cat.

So does Fat, thought Gerard. He can't stand rain. Oh Fat, where are you? As he thought this, he felt a tightness in his chest and he leant over the table to hide the heaving in his breathing.

'Where did you put her?' asked Beverley faintly.

'Parlour,' said Dymphna.

'You've put a *cow* in your parlour?' Beverley couldn't hide the astonishment and disapproval in her voice.

'Well, I wouldn't like to bring her into the kitchen,' said

Dymphna seriously. 'She might plop, you know. Cows do it all the time. Don't know any better.'

Dymphna registered the grim disbelief on the faces of her guests.

'Of course,' she went on reassuringly, 'I don't use it as a parlour any more. You might say I've converted it. It's just that I still call it the parlour. Force of habit, you might say.'

'Yes, well,' said Beverley, as if to say it was up to Dymphna to do what she liked in her own house, but she couldn't suppress one of her sniffs all the same.

'There's no need to be so prim,' Dymphna retorted, to Beverley's tone if not her words. 'It's not all that long ago that all the farming people shared their houses with the animals. They kept each other warm.'

'Really?' said Beverley weakly. Actually she knew that, but she thought it better to humour Dymphna. 'Why did you call her Dymphna?' she asked, to change the subject. Anything to make normal conversation. Anything to keep Dymphna talking and not wailing or dancing.

'After myself, of course.'

'Is that not a bit confusing?'

'No, I don't think so. I call her Dymphna. She doesn't call me anything. That's not confusing, is it? Anyway, lots of people call their children after themselves. Nobody thinks that's confusing.'

Beverley couldn't argue with the logic of this, though she felt there was something wrong with it.

'I haven't got any children,' said Dymphna sadly. 'Dymphna has, though,' she went on, cheering up. 'At least, she has a calf. Damhnait.'

'Oh? And where's Damhnait?'

'She's in the parlour too. To every cow its calf, as the saying goes.'

'I see,' said Beverley, exchanging glances with the others again. 'And what do you call the cats?' she asked politely, wishing the others would row in and help her to keep up this absurd conversation, but they all seemed to have lost their tongues.

'Pappageno,' said Dymphna. 'After the bird-catcher, you know.'

Beverley had no idea what she was referring to, but she thought it best to not to ask. 'That's a nice name. Which one is Pappageno?'

'Both of them.'

'You call *both* of them Pappageno?' Beverley was floored. How very economical Dymphna seemed to be with names!

'Yes, well, as you say yourself, it's a good name. And they both catch birds. I do love a good storm,' Dymphna went on, tucking into some more shortbread and honey. 'Don't you?'

Beverley shook her head, and looked around to see what the others were making of this conversation. Elizabeth was wriggling her toes experimentally and didn't appear to be taking much notice. Gerard was blowing his nose loudly and unnecessarily frequently. Kevin's teeth were chattering. Surely he wasn't that scared of old Dymphna? Beverley had almost begun to allow herself to believe that she was OK really.

'Put your jacket back on, Kevin,' said Beverley. 'You can't sit around in that sleeveless shirt. It's not all that warm any more.'

Kevin did as Beverley said, but his teeth didn't stop chattering.

Suddenly there was a flash, as if someone had taken a photograph, followed within seconds by a loud, crashing sound as if someone were shifting large teachests full of books about upstairs in the attic and letting them fall over.

Then the rain started, quite abruptly. It fell in sheets with a loud metallic clang. Before long, the little house was awash with hissing and singing and gushing and flushing and gurgling and splashing and drumming sounds as the rain assaulted the roof, the eaves, the guttering, the windows, the door, the rain barrel out in the garden, the garden wall, the narrow path that ran all around the house. It tried its best to get in any place it could, and soon the bandage on the kitchen window was sopping, and little trickles of water had penetrated the Sellotape seal.

The cats were wandering restlessly around the room, stalking from chair to sofa to range, their tails waving slowly in the air like drunken question marks.

Time and again the invisible photographer snapped the little group in the darkened kitchen, lighting them all for an instant with a bright, unflattering light, and then the photographer's accomplice upstairs in the attic started shoving the teachests about again. And still the house rang with the sounds of the rain.

In one of the flashes, Beverley saw that Gerard was sitting hunched over one end of the table, and Kevin was hunched at the other end, his eyes shut tight and his arms hugging his body. His teeth were still chattering, and his whole body was shivering. When the next flash came, Kevin's head was down almost on the table and he had his arms clasped defensively over it, his black elbows sticking out awkwardly like great broken wings. His stylish haircut brushed the table like a slanting curtain. He wasn't cold, it dawned on Beverley, he was scared, and it couldn't be Dymphna he was scared of, because he'd been fine until just a moment ago. It was the thunder. Kevin was afraid of thunder!

If it were Gerard, Beverley would have put her arms around his shoulders, laid her cheek against his and whispered something comforting. But Gerard was a little boy, and it was OK to mother little boys. Kevin was older. She couldn't possibly do that to him. She sat and stared miserably at his misery. If she'd been a different sort of girl, she'd have bitten her fingernails. As it was, she contented herself with twisting her hands in her lap.

One of the cats started to wail, as if that last almighty thunder-clap had been too much for it. It was a weird and chilling sound, like a baby being tortured. The sound ate into Beverley, it was so like Dymphna's wailing and yet it was a thinner, in a strange way almost more human sound.

'O-o-oh!' wailed Gerard then in desperation, and his wailing was worse even than the sound of the demented cat. Oh no! thought Beverley. Please don't all start wailing. I can't cope with any more!

Gerard wailed a second time, and then he collapsed in a fit of coughing and gasping, his bony body shaking with grief and fighting to breathe. Kevin looked up, twisting his head around without unwinding his arms. Gerard scrabbled for his inhaler and took huge, noisy lungfuls of it before his breathing settled into a normal pattern again. Gerard's face was contorted with misery. Beverley had moved over to him and was patting him repeatedly between the shoulderblades and talking softly to him, but Gerard seemed hardly to be aware of her. He was crying softly now and mumbling 'Fat, Fat,' to himself.

Kevin slowly unwrapped his arms from about his head and laid his hands firmly, palms downward, on the kitchen table, and pressed hard. Then he levered himself awkwardly into a standing position.

'Don't worry, Gerard,' he said, not looking at anyone, fixing his eyes on the backs of his hands. 'I'll find him for you.'

158

Gerard turned a peaky face streaked with tears to him and gave him a look of pure gratitude.

'You can't go out in that!' said Beverley. 'You'll be drowned. You'll catch your death. And anyway, Kevin ...' She didn't know how to finish. She didn't want to mention out loud that Kevin was terrified of thunder.

'I have to go,' said Kevin. 'Look at the state the young lad's in. I have to find his cat for him.'

Look at the state you're in yourself, Beverley thought, but didn't say.

'No, you can't, you mustn't.' Beverley surprised herself by the forcefulness of her tone. And it wasn't just that she didn't want Kevin going out in the storm. She didn't want to be left in charge either.

'I must,' said Kevin grimly.

'Take your jacket off, then,' said Beverley, with sudden inspiration, starting to pull gently at Kevin's jacket. 'Leave it here. You'll get soaked anyway, and if you leave it here, you'll have something dry to change into when you get back.' Even in a crisis, Beverley thought about the practicalities.

'Fair enough,' said Kevin, but he wasn't thinking about getting wet and having dry clothes to change into. He was clearly focused on going out into that storm.

'Good luck,' said Beverley, going with Kevin to the door.

'Thanks, Kev!' Gerard called in a hiccuppy voice from the table.

'Good on you, young Mulrooney,' said Dymphna out of the gloom and gave a low cackle of laughter.

Beverley laced her fingers quickly with Kevin's and swung his hand. He squeezed her fingers, and then he was gone.

As Beverley closed the door behind Kevin, she saw Dymphna in another lightning flash bending over Elizabeth's foot, gently applying the pink lotion. Elizabeth appeared to be asleep or at least dozing, probably the effect of the pain, Beverley thought, though how she could snooze through this racket, Beverley couldn't imagine.

Beverley sniffed as a sweet and faintly familiar smell rose into the air. It was a pleasant, happy sort of smell. What did it remind her of? Something soft and warm and gurgling. Yes – she had it now – babies. It reminded her of babies. Why, yes – Johnsons's Baby Lotion, she could swear to it! Well, that wasn't going to do much good to a twisted ankle! She smiled at the idea that Dymphna thought it might.

Beverley turned to look out of the window. A flash of lightning captured Kevin in sharp outline as he struggled to the gate, pushing against the rain and wind, his hair blown back in wet streaks from his head, and already, she could see, he was soaked to the skin. He had to fight to open the gate, but she couldn't hear its distinctive protesting squall above the roar of the storm. It was like watching a silent movie and being able to hear only the crashing of the cinema piano, not the proper sound effects of what was going on on screen. It seemed unnatural to be able to see Kevin so clearly and not be able to hear a thing to do with him. She strained to hear, as if hearing him would make the whole thing more real, more controllable, and less frightening, but the only sound she could make out above the wind and thunder was a plaintive moo from across the hall. She turned away from the window, crossing her fingers as she did so, in a helpless gesture of supplication.

Thunderclap followed upon lightning flash with monotonous

regularity, and still the rain beat relentlessly against the roof and walls. It was as if they were at sea in the little house and were being lashed about on high waves, and if it felt like that in the safety of the house, how must it feel to be out in the storm? Beverley tried to remember whether there were any trees on the island. Hedges, yes, there'd been hedges. That was much the same as trees. But were trees a good thing or a bad thing in a thunderstorm? She wasn't sure. Bad if you stood under them, because they attracted lightning, but good, perhaps, if you kept away from them, for the same reason. They were more likely to get struck than you were, because they were taller. Was Kevin taller than a hawthorn hedge? she wondered. She hoped not.

Chapter 18

THE MIRACLE

IT COULDN'T HAVE BEEN ALL THAT LONG, but Beverley was counting time in thunderbolts, and there had been plenty of them, before the garden gate squealed open (she heard it this time, in a moment of lull in the storm) and Kevin's voice came shouting, 'Open up! Open up!'

'It's Kevin,' cried Elizabeth, who had a view of the garden from her sofa. 'Oh, let him in, Beverley. He's soaked.'

Beverley ran to the kitchen door and flipped the old-fashioned rusty latch as quickly as she could. In the hall, she wrenched at the front door, but it had rained so much in the meantime that the door had swollen in its frame and she couldn't budge it. Suddenly the letter box flapped open, and she could see a slim rectangular section of Kevin's streaming face with one eye peering at her. 'You pull and I'll push,' he shouted. 'On three. Are you right?'

She nodded.

'One – two – *three*!'

At the count of three she yanked at the door and Kevin flung himself against it, and the door, which couldn't have been all that badly stuck, gave with a rush. Kevin fell inwards on top of Beverley and knocked her to the floor.

'Ouch! Get up! You're heavy!' she yelled. 'And wet!'

Beverley pushed him off and struggled to her feet. 'Did you find him?' she asked, pulling Kevin into the kitchen.

Dymphna looked up in surprise at the dripping boy. She stood up then and walked right past him, out into the hall and up the stairs.

Kevin cocked his head in a pointing gesture towards the open door of the kitchen, where Fat stood warily on the threshold, his back arched under his damp fur, looking surprisingly thin now that he was so wet, with his tail high in the air, eyeing up the resident cats, who stalked around him curiously, disdainfully, warily, but not with any overt aggression.

Gerard gave a whoop of joy, leapt to his feet, whipped Fat up into his arms out of the way of the other cats, just in case, and buried his face lovingly in his fur.

'Well done, Kevin,' said Beverley. 'Where was he?'

'Asleep under a rock, out of the rain,' said Kevin. 'Well able to look after himself, that fellow is. Gerard hadn't a right to be worrying about him at all, at all, had you, Ger?'

Gerard gave Kevin a friendly punch on the upper arm, and Kevin replied with a flap of his hand across the back of Gerard's head.

'Stoppit, you two,' said Beverley happily, hooking a hand into the crook of Kevin's elbow and giving a little swing of delight.

'Come on and get dry,' she commanded, thrilled to be giving orders now that Kevin was back and she didn't need to be in charge any more. 'I'll see if I can find you a towel or something, and take off that shirt. Slip on your jacket now before you get pneumonia.'

Dymphna reappeared, with an armful of dry towels. She handed two to Kevin, very matter-of-fact, and said: 'One to dry yourself with, one to wear. Take those pants off you before you get pneumonia.'

This sounded so like what Beverley had just said that everyone burst out laughing. Maybe Dymphna wasn't as daft as she let on. Kevin took her advice. He tied a towel about his waist like a sarong and wriggled out of his soaking jeans.

Dymphna sat down, laid a towel across her lap, and then she bent down and scooped Fat onto it and started to scrub at him with one of the remaining towels. He stretched and yawned, but made no move to discourage her.

'What's his name?' she asked.

'Fat.' It was Gerard who answered.

'What?'

'Fat – he's Fat.' Gerard was pointing at Fat.

'Oh, I wouldn't say that. He just has a lot of hair.'

Dymphna had scrubbed so hard that all Fat's cream fur had started to gleam and puff itself out in a fluffy halo around his body.

'No, he's fat all right, but what I mean is, that's his name. Fat. Short for Fat Cat.'

'Oh, I see,' said the woman thoughtfully, 'in both senses of the expression?'

'Yes,' said Gerard.

'Spoilt?'

'Ruined.'

Gerard and Dymphna smiled at one another in the soupy way that cat-lovers do when they discuss the objects of their passion.

The gaps between thunderclaps seemed to have got longer. Beverley moved to look out the window, to see whether the storm really was abating. She counted the timelag between the lightning and the thunder each time. Two seconds, two, still two, oh, three,

three, four, five, five, six, seven, nine – it sounded more removed now, a rumble only, and the flashes were softer, less garish, less alarming. But the rain was still spilling off the roof and onto the windowsill in sheets. The clouds still hung in the sky and poured water onto the garden and the path and all the landscape around for as far as she could see. There was no point in their trying to leave the cottage just yet, though it was now late into the afternoon, maybe evening. Absently, Beverley flicked her wrist to check the time, but her watch had stopped at ten to one, presumably when she had waded through the sea with Kevin.

Beverley shrugged and turned back towards the others. Another roll of thunder bellowed in the distance, like a cow in a transport truck that was already nearly at the horizon. 'The storm's moving away,' she announced. 'It'll be over any minute now.'

She was right. There were no more lightning flashes after that. The storm had passed on, leaving the house on the little island streaming but safe. It was still raining, but the rain was less frantic now. Rain fizzed along the gutters and down the drainpipe, it raced persistently down the windowpanes, but it no longer assaulted the house, as if desperate to be let in, no longer rammed itself out of the skies onto the earth with such force that it bounced back up halfway to meet itself. It hum-drummed convincingly on the slates still, but in an absentminded sort of way, as if it had given up on winning this war and had decided to be content with merely prolonging it.

The kitchen was still dark, but it was quieter now that the storm's noises had receded, and the wind that had got up as if to warn them all of the storm had died down. Beverley looked around for something to do, something to take her mind off it all. She started to gather cups to wash them up. Gerard stood up eagerly, looking for some way to help her. He found a dishcloth, and sloshed the table enthusiastically with it.

'That's nice. Thank you all,' said Dymphna, smiling benignly on the children, and appreciating the sight of her odd assortment of cups and jars ranged neatly again on the dresser.

'What about a cup of tea?' she said after a few moments. 'To celebrate.'

A cup of tea? But they'd only just washed up after the last one! This was like an even madder variation on the Mad Hatter's tea-party. Still, it was easy to make more tea, and if it kept Dymphna happy, it was worth it.

'To celebrate what, exactly?' asked Beverley cautiously.

'The storm.'

'Ah, the storm. Being over?'

'No. Being here at all.'

'What's there to celebrate about a storm?'

'Well, it's so magnificent,' explained Dymphna, flinging her arms out. For a moment, Beverley thought she was going to stand up and start her wind-dance again. 'And such a release,' Dymphna went on. 'I find it's a release. Also, it's a happening.'

'A happening?'

'Yes. Otherwise the days are so alike,' said Dymphna almost wistfully. 'Especially in the summer. You could go from one end of the week to another on this island, and not a blessed thing to differentiate one day from another.'

The children looked at each other in silence. She made life on the island sound very dull, which indeed it must be, with only cows and cats for company.

'Well, how come you live here then, all by yourself?' asked Beverley.

Kevin drew in his breath, as if to sound a warning.

'Ah well,' said Dymphna, 'ah well.' That was all. 'But what about that tea, Beverley?' she went on in a different, falsely cheerful tone. 'Didn't somebody offer to make me tea? I like a cup of tea, to celebrate.'

'Yes, certainly,' said Beverley. 'I'll make some more tea if that's what you'd like. Would you like some shortbread with it?'

'My favourite,' said Dymphna, with glee. 'How did you guess? With honey, of course.'

'Of course,' said Beverley. 'But I'm afraid there's no milk.'

'No milk?' said Dymphna. 'That's bad housekeeping, isn't it? Oh well, never mind. I'm just as happy to drink it black. In fact, I actually *prefer* it black.'

And she beamed a forgiving beam on them all.

While Dymphna munched more honey-smeared shortbread and sipped tea, Beverley took the black cotton sleeves that Kevin had ripped from his shirt and went to bandage up Elizabeth's ankle.

'The swelling's gone right down, Elizabeth,' she exclaimed, lifting Elizabeth's foot onto her lap.

Gingerly she placed a finger on the flesh and pressed. Elizabeth didn't flinch.

'Wiggle your toes,' Beverley commanded.

Obediently Elizabeth wiggled her toes.

'Turn your foot. I mean, draw a circle in the air with it.'

Elizabeth raised her foot from Beverley's lap, and, pointing her toes, described a circle in the air, swivelling her ankle as she did so.

'Does it hurt?' asked Beverley.

'No,' said Elizabeth, astonished.

'Well, the bathing would have brought the swelling down a bit,' observed Beverley, 'but I wouldn't have expected it to cure the sprain completely. Are you sure it really was sprained?' Not that it mattered. The point was that it was fine now, and that meant one thing – escape was now within their grasp.

'Sprained, strained, twisted – what do I know?' said Elizabeth, waving her foot gleefully. 'All I know is it hurt like anything. And it was all puffed up like a pigeon's chest. But suddenly it's fine. Maybe the holy well works after all. The pump's attached to it, you know.'

'Rubbish!' said Beverley.

'It's the lotion,' said Dymphna, through a mouthful of short-bread. 'I told you.'

'Rubbish!' said Beverley again, but under her breath this time.

Elizabeth swung into a sitting position and carefully placed her foot flat on the floor. She tested it by leaning on it. Not a twinge. Then she stood up slowly, half-expecting the ankle to give way. Nothing happened.

'It's a miracle!' she exclaimed, standing firmly planted on her two feet, only at an angle, because one of them was shod and the other bare.

'No, it's a *cure*,' corrected Dymphna. 'My lotion always cures people.'

Beverley scratched her head. 'It's an unexplained phenomenon,' she pronounced scientifically.

'Wow!' said Gerard, but whether in astonishment at Elizabeth's cure or at Beverley's wording was not clear.

'I'll tell you what it is,' said Kevin ruefully, fingering his amputated sleeves. 'It's a waste of my second best shirt. That's what it is.'

Chapter 19

THE BANQUET

A SORT OF PEACE HAD FINALLY DESCENDED on the kitchen. It took Beverley a moment to realise what it was: the rain had stopped at last. They were no longer being assailed by its noise. Only an occasional drip came from the roof and landed with a quiet plop in a puddle outside. Better and better – now they could get out of here. Yes!

'I think it's time we were getting on our way,' Beverley said tentatively, looking around at the others. 'We'll have to get back to the beach by the time the tide is out again, so we can walk home. What time is that by the way, Gerard?'

Gerard looked at her blankly. He'd found out about the morning tide, but it hadn't occurred to him to find out about the evening low tide for getting home again.

'Oh, it's long past low tide,' said Dymphna carelessly.

'What?' asked Beverley dismayed. They'd just got Elizabeth marching fit and it looked as though all their problems were over. And now this. Were they going to be trapped on this island for ever? Beverley looked at Dymphna with a new distrust. 'You can't mean it. What time is low tide? What time is it now anyway?'

She cast an irritated look at her stopped watch and rattled it in frustration. She tried rattling her brain too. Don't be silly, she told herself. This is not Dymphna's fault, and she is not trying to trap us here. But it did look as if they weren't going to be able to get off the island this evening. That meant they'd have to stay here overnight. Goodness knows what Dymphna would be like at night. She was weird enough in the daytime. And anyway, where would they sleep? Beverley looked doubtfully at Elizabeth's sofa. There were four of them after all, and only one sofa. She didn't fancy snuggling up with Dymphna (the cow) in the parlour. And she didn't even want to *think* what Dymphna's spare bedroom was like, if she had one.

And their parents didn't know where they were. They'd be out of their *minds*. Elizabeth had been right to want to leave them a note or tell them their plans. Why hadn't she listened to her? Why had she been so intent on punishing her parents? Just because they were a bit irritable at times. They were OK really, better than lots of parents she could mention. She was a bit irritable herself at times. And *now* look! She'd be in deep trouble after this if they stayed out all night.

'Don't know,' said Dymphna comfortably.

Nobody seemed to have a working watch, and there was no sign of a clock in this kitchen.

'But then how can you know it's too late?' asked Beverley.

'I just *do* know,' said Dymphna smugly. 'I always know when the tide's out. I feel it in my veins. And it's right in now. It won't be out again till morning. You can go and look if you like, but I'm telling you.'

The children sat in silence for a moment, taking this uncomfortable information in. Dymphna was probably right. She knew this island and its sea better than anyone. She'd be sure to know about the tide. So now what was going to happen? Their parents would have to ring the Guards. They'd be Missing Persons. There might be a child-hunt for them, with volunteers dragging the rockpools and sweeping the hills. There'd be an SOS message on the evening news. There might be a murder inquiry. Some innocent person might get arrested. It didn't bear thinking about.

'I don't suppose you have a phone?' asked Beverley, clutching at straws. A woman who kept a pet cow and calf in the parlour and thought you could cure sprained ankles with Johnson's Baby Lotion was unlikely to have a telephone.

'Oh no,' Dymphna cackled, amused at the very idea. 'I haven't even got electricity, not to mind a phone. And as you see, I have well water only.'

'Oh no!' wailed Beverley. 'What are we going to do?'

'How do you mean?' asked Dymphna.

'I mean, we're going to be stranded here. How are we going to get home? I'm hungry. And I want my mother!'

Beverley could hardly believe she'd said that last bit. It was just an infantile streak brought on by panic. She was embarrassed she'd let it slip out.

'So do I,' Gerard chipped in.

Silly child. His mother was at home in Dublin, miles away, probably listening to the Garda SOS message at this very moment.

'Well, why don't you take the boat, in that case?' asked Dymphna, as if it were the most obvious suggestion in the world.

'What boat?' snapped Beverley. 'You haven't got a phone. You haven't got electricity. You haven't even got proper running water. You're not going to tell me now that a friendly packet steamer trundles by every evening to see if you have any passengers for the mainland.'

'Arrah whisht!' said Dymphna, showing irritation for the first time. 'Of course it doesn't. But I have got a small currach.'

'A currach! One of those black beetly boats?'

'Yes.'

'Oh, but that's wonderful! Will you row us home? *Please*, Dymphna.'

'Well, now,' said Dymphna thoughtfully, 'I don't think my little curracheen would take four half-grown children, a large adult female and a cat.'

'Oh!' said Beverley, disappointed at their chance of freedom being snatched away as soon as it had appeared.

But Dymphna went on: 'I think young Mulrooney here will have to row ye.'

'Kevin, can you row?'

He didn't look like the type to be able to handle a currach.

'Yeh,' said Kevin shiftily.

'Are you sure?' Beverley was doubtful. She wanted to trust Kevin, but she had no idea how he would cope at sea in the dark.

'I'm positive. Amn't I a fisherman's son? My da, before he – well, anyway, he was a fisherman in those days. I often went out with him. I was learning. That was before.'

'But if we take the boat, how will Dymphna get it back again?' asked Elizabeth. 'It's a bit like that puzzle where the man has to get a fox, a goose and a bag of corn across a stretch of water, and can only take two items at a time. Suppose Kevin took two of us ashore, and then came back for the other one and Dymphna, and then Dymphna could row home again.'

'That's far too complicated,' said Dymphna. 'You just take the boat, and tie it up ashore. I'll walk over some day during the week at low tide and row it back later.'

The children were impressed by the sensibleness of this. Could

172

they have *imagined* that Dymphna was mad?

'If you're sure,' said Beverley politely.

'Now, did somebody say they were hungry?' asked Dymphna, ignoring Beverley's politeness.

'Well, we've only had some half-melted chocolate and a few pieces of shortbread since breakfast,' Beverley explained.

'But why didn't you say so?' Dymphna was suddenly quite the hostess.

'You said you only *had* shortbread,' said Beverley, 'and we've had some of that. We can't very well eat you out of house and home. Then *you'd* go hungry.'

'Not at all!' said Dymphna. 'It's true that I only have shortbread *in the house*,' she went on slyly, 'but outside in the back hall,' (she seemed not to count the back hall as part of the house) 'I have my messages that I picked up from the pier at Tranarone this morning. I send a list over every week with the postman, you know, and Mrs Mulrooney packs me up a cardboard box and delivers it to the pier. Very convenient.'

While Dymphna was wittering on about her grocery arrangements, and pointing out the neatness of it all, Beverley was wondering what there might be to eat. She hadn't allowed herself to think about food for some time, but now suddenly images of beef stew and fried eggs and spinach lasagne started to float before her mind's nose, so to speak.

'Oh yes,' Dymphna was saying, 'and now I come to think of it, I also have some stuff that I found on the beach this morning.'

'You found food on the beach! That must have been our supplies!' Beverley didn't know whether to be indignant or relieved.

'What supplies?' asked Dymphna, not sounding in the least

concerned. Obviously, anything she found on this island she considered as belonging to her. Did she think the fairies had left the food for her or what? And since when did the fairies pack their gifts in rucksacks? And why had she pretended earlier not to have any food apart from the shortbread? Could it be that she was lonely, and this was her way of trying to keep the children with her? And yet she'd offered them the currach to get home in. Beverley just couldn't make this strange woman out at all.

'We brought food with us for our pilgrimage,' Elizabeth explained.

'Expedition,' Beverley corrected her.

'But we left it on the beach,' Elizabeth went on. 'We thought it had been swept out to sea when the tide came in.'

'Well, isn't it lucky I found it and rescued it so?' said Dymphna complacently, as if she had done them a favour by snitching their grub, which in a sense she had. Before they had time to be angry, she went on, gleefullly: '*I* know, let's have a farewell banquet before you leave. Gerard, will you bring in the food? Beverley, find a few saucepans like a good girl.'

Really, this woman had a nerve, thought Beverley. First she stole their food and now here she was issuing party invitations on the strength of the stolen goodies.

'What's that yoke by the way?' Dymphna was pointing at the sagging garden flare, which was slouching against Elizabeth's sofa.

'It's a sort of a candle,' Beverley explained.

'Well, that's great. Can we light it? I'm out of candles, and it's getting dark in here.'

The dark that had come with the storm had never lifted, and now the dark of evening was setting in as well, and the foliage-shaded kitchen was thick with shadows. Kevin got all four rings of the gas stove going, and by its eerie light he started sorting out the food that Gerard had brought in, looking like an Oriental field-worker in his towel-sarong. He had hung his wet clothes on a hanging clothes drier that swung high above the cooker, so that they could dry in the heat given off by the cooking.

'I think it's only meant for outside,' said Beverley doubtfully, meaning the garden candle. 'It might be dangerous indoors, there might be fumes.'

'Well, then,' said Elizabeth, inspired, 'why don't we light it in the garden and have a picnic out there?'

'A picnic in the dark!' Typical Elizabeth, Beverley thought. Fanciful to the last.

'I think it's probably lighter out there than it is in here,' said Elizabeth practically. 'It stays light for ages at this time of year. And anyway, if we light the flare it won't be dark.'

'But the garden will be wet,' Beverley protested.

'I know, but we don't need to sit on the ground, like an ordinary picnic. Let's take the table and chairs outside. We can cook in here and then spread everything out on the kitchen table in the garden.'

Beverley still looked doubtful, but Elizabeth took over at this point. 'Come on, lads,' she cried, not waiting for Beverley's approval. 'Let's get this furniture shifted.' And up she hopped as if she'd never had the slightest thing wrong with her ankle and started lifting chairs.

The garden *was* wet, of course, but, as Elizabeth had said, it was both lighter and warmer than it had been in the kitchen, and they had a most glorious picnic. The sky was still filled with clouds, piled up like dirty pillows, but there was an orange glow all the same, gleaming through just at the horizon, which might have been the sunset. Elizabeth stuck the garden candle in the soaked earth, and lit it. It took immediately and lit up a small circle of rain-sparkled garden. Its reflection in the window stared back at it and enlarged the glowing circle.

Within this circle, Dymphna and the children sat around the table, illuminated by the hot and flickering light of the garden flare, their feet cold in the wet grass and their faces scorched golden-red like the faces of American Indians in the torchlight. Dymphna, still wearing her coat belted with blue twine and her sawn-off wellies, presided over the meal, graciously passing plates and doling out helpings. The evening air was seeping with the wet scent of summer flowers as they dipped fried sausages wrapped in slices of bread into tepid tinned spaghetti in tomato sauce.

'Tell us about yourself, Dymphna,' said Gerard, eating sardines with his fingers and secretly passing every second one to Fat (except it wasn't a secret at all, as everyone saw him at it, but nobody mentioned it, even though Fat had already had the best part of a tin of tuna fish).

There they went again, thought Kevin. Why couldn't these townie kids leave well enough alone and not go pestering her? Goodness knows how she might react to personal questions. He coughed loudly, partly to distract Dymphna and partly to try to warn Gerard off.

'About myself?' said Dymphna dreamily. 'Well, let's see now.'

Chapter 20

DYMPHNA'S TALE

'ONCE UPON A TIME,' DYMPHNA BEGAN.

Then she stopped and cocked her head on one side, just as the seal had done when it was looking at Beverley, and thought for a moment.

'Once upon a time,' she said again, 'there was a duckling who hated the rain. Every time it rained, she waddled for shelter. All her brothers and sisters – dozens of them there were, though actually some of them were really cousins, but nobody bothered too much in this farmyard about who exactly belonged to whom – well, all her brothers and sisters and the other ducklings in the farmyard adored the rain. They would wake up out of their sleep at the sound of it and slither into the pond and swim around ecstatically with their little beaks opening and shutting with delight. They spun around in circles and did little twirls and pirouettes, as if they were afraid they couldn't get wet enough and they wanted to be in as many places as possible at once so as to get multiple doses of raindrops. But at the first hint of rain, this little duck put her head down to make sure as much as possible of the rain ran off down her beak like a slide, and she made for cover.

'The adult ducks would quack their annoyance at her and tell

177

her to get out into the rain and not to be so unducklike, and if they found her huddled under a water-lily or behind a dock leaf during a rainstorm, they would snap at her tail feathers until she was forced out into the open again.

'Unfortunately for the duckling, there was a particularly wet summer that year of her ducklinghood, so she spent most of her time being totally miserable. One wet night when all the other ducks and ducklings were asleep and for once missing a chance to get wet, the duckling decided that she had had enough of this miserable life and that she was going to run away to a hot country. So she packed up all her belongings – which consisted of two dead caterpillars and a frog's leg that she had saved from supper that evening and a spare set of feathers her mother had given her to snuggle down into on cold nights – and off she set. She arranged the spare feathers among her own tail feathers, so that she looked like a duckling whose back half was trying to be a gosling, and she tucked the two dead caterpillars and the frog's leg under one wing, and set off at a waddle to seek her fortune and follow the sun.

'She wandered off over bogs and meadows and cornfields and across motorways and through woods and forests and housing estates, and when the morning came, she was still waddling along bravely, all alone except for the two dead caterpillars and the frog's leg. She was delighted to see the sun coming up in the morning, having travelled all night in the dark and the damp. She rewarded herself for having got so far by eating one of the caterpillars and the frog's leg. They didn't taste as fresh and juicy as the caterpillars and frog's legs she had had the previous evening, naturally enough, considering they had travelled all night in the duckling's oxter.

'She waddled along a bit more in the sunshine after that, but by now she was starting to feel very weary. She wondered how far she had come, but she had no way of knowing. She wondered if she was in a hot country yet – she didn't know that Ireland was an island and that she would have to travel over the sea before she had any chance of getting to a hot country.

'As she waddled along more and more slowly, wondering where she was and how far from the tropics, she met a man carrying a load of hay. The hay looked soft and warm and sweet and inviting, and as soon as she saw it, the duckling thought that she would like to sleep in it.

'She asked the man if he would barter a load of his hay for a dead caterpillar, but the man just laughed and laughed and didn't even answer her.

'So the duckling waddled sadly and wearily along some more, and then she met a woman driving a mule. The mule was pulling a cart full of sticks. The sticks looked like a very uncomfortable sort of a place for a duckling to sleep, but by now she was so tired she thought she could sleep on a load of sticks, so she asked the woman if she would barter part of her load of sticks for a dead caterpillar, but the woman got such a shock to hear a duck talking that she didn't wait to hear the bargain she was offering. She just gee'ed her mule up into a canter and trundled off out of earshot with her cartload of sticks.

'By now the duck was desperate for someplace to sleep, but still she could find nowhere suitable, so when she met a cement mixer coming along the road she didn't even ask the driver if she could have some of his cement to sleep on, she just made one huge effort and flew up and in at the mouth of the cement mixer.

'When she raised her wings to flap them so that she could make her valiant little flight, of course the second dead caterpillar fell out of her oxter, so there was her lunch gone. But the little duck was by now too tired to care about food.

'Inside the cement mixer, she flew round and round a bit to get her bearings, and she soon realised that this was no place for a duckling to be trying to get some sleep. But she was so desperately sleepy that eventually her little wings stopped flapping and she fell down into the cement mixture and sank right into the middle of it. The blades of the cement mixer turned the cement relentlessly, and the duckling with it, like a rather large plum in a cake. Up and down and round and round the cement mixer she went, completely coated in cement, but the little duckling didn't know a thing about it, for she was by now fast asleep. Presently the cement mixer came to a halt, and the cement was poured out at the back of the machine, into a pit on a building site. When the movement of the machine stopped, the duckling woke up and felt herself being slowly catapulted through the air and into this pit.

'Her sleep had refreshed her, so she was able to gather enough strength to pull herself out of the pit, but of course she was completely covered from beak to spare tail feathers with cement. She didn't see any way to get the sticky stuff off, so the duckling resigned herself to a new life as a statue.

'She stood very still and allowed the cement to dry, which it began to do very rapidly, and before very long it had dried into a duckling-shaped statue. The duckling was rather pleased with her new life, and she stood still by the side of the building site all day – for of course she had no option – and waited for something to happen. Being a statue had its advantages, she soon began to realise. For a start, statues don't need to eat or drink, so she would never again have to worry about being hungry or thirsty. And as to sleep, a statue's whole life could be looked upon as one long sleep, and she would never again have to worry about finding somewhere to lay her weary head.

'That evening, one of the building workers noticed the little duckling statue by the side of the building site and wondered where it had come from. It didn't appear to belong to anybody, so he took it home with him and put it in his garden. And the little duckling statue still stands in the building worker's garden, rain or shine, and from that day to this, the duckling has never again had to worry about the rain, for, imprisoned inside the concrete, she never gets wet. In fact, the only sorrow in the duckling's life is that occasionally she gets an itch at the end of her beak, and, being a statue, she is unable to lift her wing and scratch it. But that is a small price to pay for security and protection from the weather.

'So, if ever you are walking past a garden and notice a duckling-shaped statue, especially if it is one with a rather disproportionately large tail, you might give the little duckling a wave and wish her good day.'

The children clapped when she finished, and Dymphna stood up and took a little bow, holding out the hem of her raincoat with the tips of her middle fingers again.

'That was a cool story,' said Gerard, 'but why don't you tell us about yourself?'

Oh no, thought Kevin, not again!

'Ah, but that *is* my story,' said Dymphna, picking through the peanuts for the ones with little bits of roasted skin still on them. 'When you tell a story, it's your story. Your telling it makes it yours. And every time you tell a story, you're telling people something about yourself. Didn't you know that?'

'Oh!' said Gerard, because suddenly he did know, suddenly he understood.

'Here, have one of these, Gerard,' said Kevin, shoving a saucepan full of crisps under his nose. (They'd had to use saucepans, as Dymphna didn't seem to have many bowls or dishes.) 'Take a few,' he said, rattling the saucepan, trying desperately to get Gerard to shut up, stop probing.

Beverley opened the tinned fruit and passed it around, still in the tin and they all spooned it up gratefully in turn. Kevin tore bananas off the bunch and tossed one to everyone. Elizabeth helped everyone to biscuits. Dymphna proffered more shortbread, but nobody could look at another bit.

'How are you going to steer in the dark, Kevin?' asked Gerard, after they'd finished their meal and started to think about leaving Lady Island. 'Are you sure it's safe?'

'Safe as safe can be,' said Kevin reassuringly. 'There are no currents or rocks in the bay, and all I have to do is head for the lights of Tranarone. We can't go wrong, I promise you. As long as everyone sits still and you keep that animal under control.'

That animal was curled up on Gerard's bony knees, snoring, and looking as if he couldn't possibly cause trouble if he tried.

'Good old Fat!' said Elizabeth unexpectedly, and leaned over to stroke his dirty-cream ears. 'I'm sure he'll be as good as gold.'

Gerard stared at his cousin in amazement. There was certainly nothing like a feed for putting Elizabeth in a good mood. He couldn't remember her saying a single kind word about Fat ever before. Beverley put a motherly arm around Gerard's shoulders and gave him a friendly little squeeze. Gerard's amazement grew. They were starting to like him!

'Before you go,' Dymphna said, as they were clearing up and putting the furniture back in the house, 'there's one thing I have to ask you to promise me.'

Uh-oh, thought Beverley. Now what? Just as they were almost free.

'If you promise, I'll tell you where the boat is.'

'OK,' said Kevin. 'What's the promise?'

'Don't tell them,' Dymphna hissed, gripping Kevin's arm.

'Who? What?'

'Them,' insisted Dymphna. 'Anyone. They're all the same. It doesn't matter who.'

'But what are we not to tell them?' Kevin asked, though he knew, really. Dymphna didn't want people knowing about her crazy spells. Not that she was all that crazy really. She was quite sane in lots of ways.

'That you saw me. I'm not supposed to be here, you know.'

'But Dymphna,' said Kevin gently, 'everyone knows you're here. They all know you in Tranarone. You come over for your messages. The postman calls with your mail.'

'Oh, yes, I know, I know, but don't tell them anyhow,' she insisted. 'Not officially. *Please*, Kevin, please.'

Dymphna's voice wobbled. She was pleading with Kevin, and she sounded close to tears. She knew people knew she was here, of course she did, but what she was really asking was that the children wouldn't talk about her to the people on the mainland. All she really wanted was to be left alone. She was terrified that they would come and take her away.

'It's not my island,' she said. 'It's not my house. Some rich person owns it. I know they want me out, even though I pay my rent. They can't get me out, though, sure they can't, Kevin?'

'No,' said Kevin, 'of course they can't, not if you pay your rent,' though in fact he hadn't a clue whether they could or not. 'Look, don't worry, Dymphna, we won't say a thing, not a word. I promise.'

'What about them?' Dymphna asked, still talking to Kevin, but waving her arm at the others. 'Those city children?'

'They won't either, not a whisper,' said Kevin. 'We promise, don't we everyone?'

'Oh Dymphna,' said Gerard, 'we wouldn't *dream* of it!'

'What about the curly one?' Dymphna asked Gerard. 'She looks as if she might tell.'

'Beverley? No way, she won't, will you, Bev?'

'No,' said Beverley. 'No, definitely not.' And she meant it. Poor Dymphna, living her funny life out here on the island, in precarious isloation, scared to death of being evicted, or worse.

'Are you sure?' asked Dymphna, looking pleadingly at Beverley. 'I don't want to go into one of those places, you know,' and she tapped her forehead.

'No, I promise, I won't tell a soul you're here or that we met you or anything, really and truly I won't, and neither will Elizabeth or Gerard.'

'Right so,' said Dymphna, with a sudden beam, and she explained to Kevin where the boat was stashed. She produced a battery-operated torch to light their way, and she stood at the gate, the garden candle flickering behind her and seeming to cast a nimbus around her, and waved them all goodbye. The Pappagenos wove in and out of the candle's orangey light, only the tips of their tails visible, wavering as they tiptoed disdainfully around the unpleasantly damp grass.

The children stood at the gate for a moment and waved back at Dymphna. Then Kevin swung the torch to light up the daisy-sprinkled trail back to the beach, and they were off. The daisies had all curled up for the night, but they still showed white against the grey-blue evening grass, in the light of the torch, like Hansel and Gretl's pebbles gleaming in the moonlight.

At the beach they found the currach where Dymphna had said it would be and clambered aboard. As Kevin pushed it out to sea and leapt on board himself at the last minute, the others hunkered together and sat as still as they could, talking in low whispers. Kevin stood in the boat and looked down ruefully at his jeans, streaming for the third time today. He might as well have spent the day in swimming togs.

As the little craft pulled away from the shore, Kevin rowing strongly and confidently, the children could just make out the point of light that marked Dymphna's garden, and they fancied they could see a shadowy figure still at the gate, still waving slowly as they plashed and rocked their way out to sea and made for the string of lights on the far shore that identified Tranarone, civilisation, parents, home.

Chapter 21

AFTER AND BEFORE

'WHAT I DON'T UNDERSTAND,' Elizabeth was saying, 'is how my ankle got better so quickly.'

It was three weeks later. There'd been plenty of trouble when the children got home. The local sergeant had questioned a few people, and the children's parents were in a right state about them. They'd been lectured and hugged and grounded in that order. But it had all blown over by now. And they hadn't squealed on Dymphna. They just said they'd missed the tide and then they'd found this boat and borrowed it.

Elizabeth and Gerard were leaving Tranarone the next day, and Kevin and Beverley had come to say goodbye. They were all gathered around the round, brown table in the Ryans' holiday bungalow kitchen.

'It must have been only slightly twisted, Elizabeth,' Beverley insisted. 'You probably thought it was worse than it really was, because you'd had trouble with that ankle before, and you were expecting the worst.'

'No,' said Elizabeth. 'It was genuine agony, I tell you. Really bad. And then suddenly it wasn't any more.'

'Well, it can't have been the Johnson's Baby Lotion, can it?' Beverley reasoned.

'No,' Elizabeth agreed reluctantly, 'but it might have been the water from the holy well.'

'Ah rubbish!' said Beverley vehemently. 'Even if that sort of thing does work, surely you would have to know you were doing it. You'd have to pray and concentrate on it and that sort of thing.'

'No, I don't think so,' said Elizabeth. 'I think the whole point about a miracle is that it's – well, *undeserved*, if you see what I mean.'

Beverley shook her head. She couldn't, simply couldn't, accept that it had been a miracle. Nothing would ever convince her.

'It doesn't really matter, does it?' said Gerard. 'The main thing is that the ankle got better. What difference does it make how?'

The two girls looked at the small boy pityingly. He was obviously too young to appreciate what was really important in life.

'I mean,' Gerard went on stoutly, 'you might say it was a miracle that Fat turned up, but I don't care what it was, just so long as he did.'

He gave Fat a hug as he said this, and Fat grudgingly put up with it.

'That's completely different, Gerard,' said Beverley, but patiently. 'The chances were that Fat would turn up anyway. There's nothing miraculous about that. Not even anything vaguely mysterious.'

'But it *felt* like a miracle to me,' Gerard argued.

'Feelings don't come into it,' said Beverley, putting on her scientist's voice again.

'And what about my asthma?' asked Gerard. 'Has anyone noticed that I haven't had a single attack in three weeks, since the day on the island, in fact?'

The others looked at Gerard in amazement. They hadn't

noticed, but now that he said it, of course he was right.

'Well then it can't have been the well water, or the lotion either,' said Kevin, going back to the earlier part of the conversation. 'I think it was Dymphna. You can see why people think she's a witch, if she goes around curing people like that.'

'They think she's a *witch*!' said Beverley indignantly. She didn't know whether to be more outraged at people's ignorance in believing in such nonsense or angry that they should think such an unflattering thing about their friend. Since they'd left the island and looked back on their adventures there, they had got fonder and fonder of Dymphna, and they'd completely forgotten how scared of her they'd all been at the time. 'That's absurd!'

'Yeh, but there it is,' said Kevin. 'That's why she lives out there on that island, away from people. They would give her an awful time if she lived in the village. They did in the past. They hounded her out to the island. And that's why nobody ever goes out there. They're afraid of her. And you heard what she said. The people who own the island are trying to get rid of her, and if they do manage to evict her, what's going to happen to her? She's afraid they're going to put her into one of those hospitals.'

'Just because she's a bit peculiar?' asked Beverley. 'They can't do that!'

'Well, she's more than a *bit* peculiar,' said Kevin, remembering the wailing and the dancing.

'But Dymphna's a sweetie,' said Beverley. 'She's no more a witch than you are, Kevin.'

'I thought you said she was weird!' said Gerard indignantly.

'I never did,' said Beverley. 'That was Elizabeth who said that.'

'Well,' said Elizabeth, 'I didn't mean it unkindly. But she is pretty eccentric, you must admit, drinking her tea black rather than milk the cow! I mean, I *ask* you.'

'She's probably just leaving the milk for the calf,' said Kevin. 'That's just good farming.'

'Yes, but those names. And keeping the cow in the parlour,' Elizabeth went on. She rather liked the idea that Dymphna might be a witch – the good sort, of course. 'And the wailing, remember the wailing?'

Everyone remembered the wailing. It brought them out in goosebumps again, just thinking about it. But did it mean Dymphna was mad, or mad enough to be put away? Probably not. What harm was it doing?

'The thing I really don't understand is about the stories,' said Kevin. 'I mean, where did they come from, and why did we tell them? I never told a story in my life before, did you?'

'It's something to do with the island,' said Gerard. 'It makes people tell stories. It must be a story island. And remember what Dymphna said? Everyone tells their *own* story.'

'What do you mean, Gerard?' asked Beverley. Really the little lad was losing the run of himself. Maybe he'd got too much sun.

'Well, take Dymphna's story, for example,' said Gerard, getting enthusiastic now. 'The duckling who didn't like the rain. Well, that's really Dymphna, you see. She's different, she's peculiar, she doesn't do the sort of things everyone else does and like the things other people like. She's like the duckling, and like the duckling, she ran away, looking for somewhere new to live, where she would be able to be different in peace. And then the duckling got covered over in cement and that made her happy, remember? That's what Dymphna wants, to be safe and protected and out of the rain, only the rain you see in the story means the way ducklings are supposed to live, so in Dymphna's case it means the way other

189

people live, all ordinary, like us, with lawnmowers and insurance policies and school uniforms and everything, see?'

'Golly!' said Beverley. 'I think you're right, Gerard. How did you work all that out?'

'Well, I just *liked* her so much,' said Gerard. 'I knew she wasn't bad, even if she might be a bit mad. And I just kept thinking and thinking about it, and wondering about her and trying to work out why she behaved so oddly some of the time and so normally the rest of the time, and I thought she must have been afraid of something. And then she made us promise not to tell about her, because she was afraid of whoever owns the island trying to get rid of her. I think she must be scared of people coming to the island, in case they're coming to take her away, and so when she saw us right there in her kitchen, she must have been terrified, and so as soon as she got a chance to get away from us, she started that awful wailing – I said at the time it was because she was upset. It sounded like ... like *despair*! And I felt so sorry for her when I heard it, and then I thought, gee, she really thinks she's blown it now, because now we all know how nutty she is, and she's worse off than ever, and so then she tried to behave more normally, and she did some of the time, but she couldn't keep it up, because she's so used to living on her own and doing whatever she feels like. But then she needed us to understand how threatened she felt, how much she needed to be protected, and so she told us the story, like a sort of code so we'd understand. Only she didn't give us the key to the code, because that's not how stories work. You have to work them out for yourself and make your own sense of them, so then she had to make us promise too, you see, in case we didn't understand the code.'

'I think you're right, Gerard,' said Elizabeth. 'Wow! I didn't know you could be so smart.'

'Oh gee,' said Gerard, blushing and hiding his face in Fat's fur.

'Poor Dymphna,' said Beverley.

'Yeah, poor old thing,' said Elizabeth, and the others nodded in agreement.

'Anyways, we better get a move on,' said Kevin after a while. 'It's teatime. Are you ready, Beverley?'

Kevin and Beverley stood up to go. Beverley kissed Elizabeth and gave Gerard a hug. He was embarrassed and delighted at the same time, but he tried not to squirm too much. Kevin shook hands with them both and said 'Pssst!' loudly in Fat's ear, by way of farewell.

Beverley and Kevin left the others to their packing and wandered along the sand-strewn tarmac in the direction of Kevin's mother's shop.

'What did you mean by before, Kevin?' Beverley asked.

'What?'

'Your dad. On the island you said he was a fisherman, but that was before. Before what?'

'Oh, that before,' said Kevin with a shrug. He didn't say any more for a while. Then he looked out to sea, to Lady Island, lying innocently in the bay, and said, 'Before he left. Before he went away. Before he *emigrated*, you could say.' And he shrugged again and kicked a stone with the side of his foot.

'You mean, he left you?' said Beverley softly.

'Yes, me, my mother, my brothers and sisters.' Kevin didn't look at her as he said this. 'I mean, he sends us birthday cards and he comes to visit sometimes, but he's got a new life now, beyond in England.'

'That story about the mermaids,' Beverley went on. 'It was

really your own story, then, just like Gerard said we all told our own stories?'

'Sort of, I suppose so,' said Kevin, kicking the stone again, this time more savagely. 'We all told our own story, didn't we?'

'Mmm, yes, I think you're right. Except Elizabeth. Not so much anyway. That story was for us all, wasn't it?'

'Yes, well, I suppose stories are like that, aren't they? Wherever they come from, they're for us all really, once you tell them.'

'Once you tell them. Twice you don't,' said Beverley, cryptically.

'Well, twice upon a time would never do, would it?' said Kevin.

'No, I suppose not,' said Beverley, and she knew that three weeks ago she could never have had such a peculiar conversation, but that was before ... before everything, well, just before.